"I wasn't starin̶̶̶̶̶̶̶̶̶̶̶̶̶̶̶̶̶̶̶̶̶̶̶̶̶̶̶̶̶̶̶̶̶̶̶̶̶ class," Conner stated

"You were. There's a girl at the cheerleading practices who looks exactly like her, only with shorter skirts and more makeup," Tia said.

"They're the twins I told you about a few days ago," he said unenthusiastically. Some part of Conner wanted to riff on the absurdity of the Barbie twins and the evil they and their kind represented to high schools all over the country. He could go off.

But he just didn't have it in him.

Barbie Two was proving surprisingly hard to mock and ridicule. He hated when people did that. He'd counted on her being stupid and dull witted. He'd wanted her to say "like" every third word. He'd wanted her to write her essay about her first pet, a poodle named Fluffy. He'd wanted her to shrivel and writhe under his condescending gaze.

Perhaps most of all, he'd wanted her to continue to wear cloying outfits like that awful yellow dress she'd worn the first day and not sensible things like well-fitting jeans and V-necked T-shirts, so he wouldn't have to consider the fact that she was actually very pretty.

Over all, Elizabeth Wakefield was turning out to be a huge disappointment.

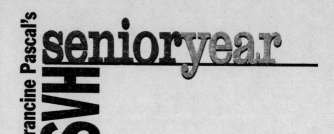

Francine Pascal's

**SVH** senioryear

# Can't Stay Away

### CREATED BY
# FRANCINE PASCAL

BANTAM BOOKS
NEW YORK • TORONTO • LONDON • SYDNEY • AUCKLAND

# RL 6, age 12 and up

CAN'T STAY AWAY

*A Bantam Book / February 1999*

*Sweet Valley High® is a registered trademark of Francine Pascal.*
*Conceived by Francine Pascal.*
*Cover photography by Michael Segal.*

Produced by 17th Street Productions,
a division of Daniel Weiss Associates, Inc.
33 West 17th Street
New York, NY 10011.

ISBN: 0-553-49234-9

*Published simultaneously in the United States and Canada*

Bantam Books are published by Bantam Books, a division of Random
House, Inc. Its trademark, consisting of the words "Bantam Books" and
the portrayal of a rooster, is Registered in U.S. Patent and Trademark
Office and in other countries. Marca Registrada. Bantam Books, 1540
Broadway, New York, New York 10036.

PRINTED IN THE UNITED STATES OF AMERICA

OPM    0 9 8 7 6 5 4 3 2 1

*To Laurie and Richard Wenk*

# Elizabeth Wakefield's New School Year's Resolutions

I will not get straight A's this year. It's bad for a person's image. Or at least I won't get all A's second semester. Or if I do, I won't tell anyone about it.

I will not give Jessica advice, no matter how horrendously wrong she is. (Unless, of course, she's going to jump off the roof. Or go out with a jerk, or fail an exam, or wear that grotesque dark green nail polish with the matching lipstick.)

I will not get back together with Todd Wilkins, no matter how tempted I am. I'm moving on.

I will not hate my job at House of Java or the owner, Mrs. Scott, the cheapest human being in America.

I will continue to hide sugar packets just to bug her. (I still can't believe she actually counts them.)

I will continue to be taller than Jessica and still weigh one pound less.

I'll dress more sexily. If I can do it and still wear sneakers.

I will reappraise some of my decisions about sex, though I'm probably not going to do _it_.

I will not give constructive criticism to anyone anymore, no matter how much Enid needs it.

I will put the earthquake behind me, but I'll never forget it.

And most of all, I will always remember Olivia.

# Jessica Wakefield's Senior Year Resolutions

I will clean my room once a week. Okay, let's be realistic. Every other week.

I will read that book Elizabeth bought me six months ago — <u>Twin Rivalry: The Good, the Bad, and the Ugly</u> — if for no other reason than I'm sick of her asking whether I've "gotten to it."

I won't eat at McDonald's or Taco Bell unless Lila offers to pay, in which case it doesn't really count.

I will do my homework unless there's something better to do.

I will continue to weigh one pound less than Elizabeth.

I will . . .

Wait a second. Why am I bothering with this list? It's not like I'm actually going to <u>do</u> any of these things, so what's the point?

Sweet Valley High. <u>Sweet</u> Valley. After twelve mind-numbing years in the El Carro school district of southern California, I'm spending my senior year at Sweet Valley High. For the rest of my life I'll have a diploma from Sweet Valley High. As long as I live, I'll be getting notices of homecomings and pep rallies and reunions from my pals at Sweet Valley High.

I picture the walls of the place painted cotton-candy pink and the cafeteria serving fresh-fruit smoothies all day long. I picture all the girls as blondes wearing pastel colors with names that end in <u>ie</u>. I picture a final exam on cute, rhyming school slogans they've forced us to memorize. I picture a perfectly round sun shining brightly over tall oaks and a fountain sprinkling happily in the courtyard. I picture group hugs.

I don't picture me.

While I'm getting dressed, I rummage through my drawer for my biggest, most disreputable pants and my rattiest T-shirt. Then I root through my closet for my oldest, heaviest boots. As an afterthought I grab a tired-looking overcoat from the hook.

Maybe if I get really, really lucky, it will rain.

# MELISSA FOX

I hate new things. I'm sorry, but I do. I hate change, I hate losing, and I hate surprises of any kind. Is it any shock, then, that this summer has been a living hell for me? First the earthquake, which all but destroyed my house. My summer plans were ruined when my parents carted me and my sister off to Maryland to stay with my freaky aunt Judy. Then I found out about school. For the first time in three years I was actually looking forward to high school, and then I find out the damage from the quake was so bad, the school board was sending five hundred of us to Sweet Valley High and the rest to the high school in Big mesa.

In less than an hour I'm going to be walking the unfamiliar halls of Sweet Valley High, being stared at by strange faces and hating every second of it.

Thank God I still have Will.

# ELIZABETH WAKEFIELD

## 7:42 A.M.

This isn't what I expected. I've imagined getting ready for my first day of senior year many times, but I never pictured it in a chintz-filled guest room in Lila Fowler's mansion, where my parents wander the halls like zoned-out political refugees. I can't seem to find any of my stuff, even though I know I unpacked everything I have. But I shouldn't complain about the fact that some member of the Fowlers' household staff launders my clothes practically before I've taken them off. That doesn't exactly make you want to weep for me, does it?

My third-grade teacher used to say, "Don't be part of the problem; be part of the solution." I took it to heart. I guess that's why I haven't really wanted to talk to anyone about how strange this is for me and how desperately I want to go home. I've been through so little compared to so many people. I have <u>nothing</u> to complain about. I guess that's why I'm wearing a yellow minidress today even though my mood is so gray.

# JESSICA WAKEFIELD
## 7:58 A.M.

I'm late. My sister is clicking around the hallway, making little sighing and huffing noises, and I'm still searching for my powder blue platforms. So Elizabeth the Good will be two minutes late to her "Welcome to Sweet Valley" orientation schmooze-a-thon. So she won't be able to meet and greet every single El Carro student. So she'll give one less meaningful gaze as some newcomer tells their particular story of earthquake woe.

I can't take another fuzzy-feelings session on that subject. I just can't. What's the deal with the "talking always makes you feel better" rule? Who came up with that anyway?

I know exactly what would make _me_ feel better. Finding my shoes.

# CHAPTER 1
## All's Fair in High School

Conner McDermott glanced warily at the throng of students crowding the entrance hall of Sweet Valley High. He knew there was supposed to be some kind of orientation for El Carro students. If he followed the lost-looking kids or, better yet, the perky-looking ones with the big buttons that read Welcome to Sweet Valley High! he'd probably find the way.

The walls did not appear to be pink, at least not in this part of the school. They were cinder block, just like at El Carro, covered by multiple shiny coats of mayonnaise-colored paint. The endless rows of lockers were a soulless gray-green, just like all lockers.

He scanned the crowds for a familiar face. Andy's unbrushed hair or Tia's precoffee snarl would be a welcome sight right now. Instead his eyes landed on two girls hurrying up behind him.

"Oh, man," he murmured, getting out of their way. They were too much, really. He almost wanted to laugh. A matched set of perfect-looking

1

aqua-eyed blondes, one in sunny yellow and the other in baby blue. Twins. *Tweedledumb and Tweedledumber,* he thought bleakly. Poster girls for Sweet Valley High.

The one in blue swept her gaze over his boots, overcoat, and scowl, summing him up instantly and casting him aside with a look that said, "You don't belong here." The look was right.

Conner walked down the hall, suddenly wanting some air. At the end of a long corridor he spotted an exit door glowing with a square panel of sunlight. He pushed through it, blinking in the brightness.

"No way." He said it out loud as he stared at the picturesque courtyard and its bubbling fountain. It was a nightmare come true.

He wheeled around and pushed back into the dark hallway. It sure seemed like someone up there was having a little laugh at his expense.

At the end of the hall he spotted a familiar face.

"Tia," he called, fighting the temptation to actually run over to where she was standing.

"Hey," she said, her strained expression transforming into an utterly comforting smile. He'd always loved that smile. It wasn't that it was so stunningly beautiful—not in the standard sense anyway. Her two front teeth overlapped slightly, and she had a deep dimple under the left corner

2

of her mouth. But her smile was so open and welcoming, so totally unself-conscious, that even when Tia tried to be cool and glamorous, it gave her away. He loved the fact that she was literally incapable of the phony crap so many girls pulled.

"We're strangers in a strange land," he said, glancing over her somewhat tattered boot-cut jeans and her black baby tee.

"Yeah. And you've got the shell-shocked look to prove it," she said, gathering her long, uncooperative dark hair over one shoulder.

"I just walked through the door at the end of this hall and there was a courtyard and a fountain," he said with obvious disgust.

She laughed. "Conner, only you would find that cause for alarm."

"Come on, Tee," he said irritably. "You know what I mean. This place is so fake. So perfect. I just about collided with this pair of matching Barbie dolls who probably have an IQ of a hundred points between them. One of them glared at me like I had just mugged her grandmother or something. I can't take these shallow, judgmental types, you know? It's like they're appraising your entire existence by the shoes you wear."

Tia smiled again, but this one was more complex. "Judgmental types, huh?" She held his glance for an extra moment. "Takes 'em to know 'em."

\*       \*       \*

Melissa Fox carefully folded her cheerleading sweater into locker number 379. Those were her three favorite numbers, which she took as a good omen. She'd had the sweater since September of sophomore year, when she'd become the youngest member of the El Carro varsity squad. Last year, when she'd been voted captain, she'd been presented with a new sweater that spelled out her title in gold thread over the breast. But she couldn't bear to throw out her old good-luck sweater, so she'd actually embroidered *Captain* on the old one herself and shoved the new one to the back of her closet. She hadn't mentioned that to anyone, of course. She didn't want her friends thinking she was a complete freak. So she was superstitious— was that so wrong?

She'd already fitted the locker door with a mirror and three pictures she always kept close: the one of her mom and dad on their wedding day, the one of her and Will before their junior prom, the one of her brother and sister the Halloween she'd turned five. A lot of people might say that being born on Halloween was unlucky, but she disagreed.

She took a quick glance in the mirror before slamming the door. She had three minutes to find Will before calculus. He had history this period— she'd already memorized his schedule. After an orientation, a tour, an assembly, and an uncountable number of strangers, she was relieved to finally be turning back to the comfort of binders and text-books.

Will's locker was 581, none of her favorite numbers. He turned to look at her, and she noticed immediately the tension in his face.

"What's up?" she asked him.

"This sucks, Liss," he said, shutting his locker with a bang.

She tugged on his sleeve. "Could you elaborate?"

He shrugged her off impatiently. "This was supposed to be our time. Seniors. We waited three years for our chance, and now we're demoted to new-kid status."

She wanted to touch his face. She loved the way his gold-brown hair had grown long this summer, the way it curled sweetly around his collar. But he needed space at the moment. "More football stuff?"

"Yeah. More. I'm getting hazed by guys who are supposed to be my teammates. I'm getting taunted by Ken Matthews's offensive line. These guys are more loyal than dogs. Even the coach himself laid it out for me at the end of training camp yesterday. He said Ken's first-string. That's that."

"So you'll start out second-string," she said reasonably.

He shook his head in disgust. "You obviously don't get it, Liss. I'm not going to get a division one scholarship as a second-stringer."

When he got like this, she knew how to handle it. She was quiet. She waited. He wanted to be provoked, and he would try to provoke her. She wouldn't take the bait.

"What about you?" he demanded angrily. "You think you're going to be captain of the cheerleading squad this year? No chance. Some girl named Jessica Wakefield already owns the title. It doesn't matter how good you are."

The bell was going to ring in ten seconds. She had ten seconds to diffuse this tirade. She shifted her books in her arms. She knew when he needed comfort, and she knew when he needed something else.

"The Sweet Valley crowd has what we want," she said slowly. "Until we take it. All's fair in high school." She focused her gaze on a slender brunette in a very short skirt. "I haven't met Jessica Wakefield yet. But I'm not afraid of her."

Blond. Brunette. Brunette. Blond. Tall. Taller. Not so tall. The possibilities seemed endless as Jessica scanned the crowd of El Carro guys seated at the back of her American history class. She picked a seat two rows ahead that afforded the best view.

Everybody in the senior class had been moaning and groaning for the last few weeks of summer about the El Carro invaders, but couldn't they see the obvious upside? (Besides Mr. Cooper, the new vice principal, and the guidance counselor being stuck in a trailer so their offices could be used for classroom space?) What intelligent Sweet Valley High girl could fail to see the benefit of this influx of supremely datable guys when they most needed them?

Cute. Cuter. Seriously good-looking . . .

And there he was. Mr. Drop-dead Gorgeous. The guy was over six feet tall—she could tell that much by the way he was squeezed into the desk—and had tousled, dark blond hair.

*Look up,* she commanded him mentally. *I want to see your eyes.* He glanced at the blackboard. Gray-blue with little halos of yellow around his pupils. Beautiful. His eyes fell on her, but she didn't turn away. Slowly she raked a hand through her chin-length hair and smiled. He looked down again.

*Oh, well.* He was a senior if he was in this class. By the look of him, she guessed he was an athlete, maybe a football player. But his appearance didn't shout *jock* in an obvious way. He wasn't too bulky. He wasn't a thumbhead, as Elizabeth called sportsmen of the no-neck variety. He wasn't the sweatpants type who always wore a baseball cap with an obsessively curled brim. Instead he wore a blue oxford, neither pressed nor too wrinkly, and a pair of jeans, just the right shade. Suddenly Jessica was desperate to get a look at his feet. Shoes were the most telling part of any guy's wardrobe.

Mr. Crowley was talking about mercantilism now. That seemed like a lot of syllables for the first day of school, but she wrote it down anyway. Jessica angled her chair so that she could still glance at the back of the room. Mr. Beautiful was listening carefully, taking the occasional note. His hands were nice, slender but not effeminate. He was left-handed, she noticed, trying to remember what that *Mademoiselle* article had said about lefties. Lefties were creative, she remembered. Artistic or something.

She glanced at the clock, never quite taking her eyes off him. No girl without great peripheral vision could hope for any serious romantic conquests.

He was tough, this guy, refusing to give her a second glance. Maybe he hadn't seen her smile at him. Or maybe he had and just thought she was a troll. She'd give him ten more minutes to look up. Mr. Crowley droned, and Amy Sutton botched the answer to a question on colonial economies.

*Okay, ten more,* Jessica thought generously. Her ego was starting to bruise, so she decided to distract herself. She started a list of stuff she needed to remember for the cheerleading meeting that afternoon. She'd go from there to a four-hour shift at Healthy, the New Agey place where she spent twelve hours a week helping gullible customers to her vast pretended knowledge of herbal remedies. She made a note to tell her mom she wouldn't be home for dinner. *For the third night in a row,* a voice in her head noted absently.

It took Mr. Beautiful until the last two minutes of class, that final restless stretch when the teacher loses control, if he or she ever had it. Just when Jessica was beginning to think the guy was a lost cause and maybe she didn't look quite as good in blue as she thought she did, he looked up.

His glance was quick, but thorough. She waited until the last possible second to catch his eye.

*Gotcha,* she thought triumphantly as she gathered up her books.

Elizabeth made it through orientation and an all-school assembly before her luck ran out. She couldn't have hoped for much more than that.

He was standing in a small clump of guys— Aaron Dallas, Max Waters, and Jake Collins—near the entrance to the cafeteria. He'd be sort of hard to avoid if she felt like eating today. Pretty much the second she was through the doors, he spotted her and walked over.

The place was a madhouse. The cafeteria was always noisy, so an extra hundred-plus seniors gave it roughly the volume of a rock concert. She could see that they'd beefed up the serving staff and added extra tables around the perimeter. Students were spilling out into the courtyard, where more tables had been added. *It's a good thing it rains so rarely,* she thought, her brain having shifted to autopilot.

"Hey, Liz," Todd said, stepping close enough to be heard. Of course Elizabeth had known this moment would arrive. She had even planned, word for word, what she would say to him when they came face-to-face after almost three months apart. But now that her ex-boyfriend was actually standing less than two feet away, Elizabeth's prepared speech abandoned her and a small flutter started in her stomach.

He was irritatingly good-looking. A summer at a North Carolina basketball camp hadn't changed that. He was deeply tanned and strong, maybe even a little taller than he'd been in June. His normally dark hair was cut short and tinged blond by the sun. He smelled faintly spicy—like nutmeg-scented shaving cream. She could practically feel his breath on her hair.

*Be cool, Wakefield.* "Todd, hi!" The greeting came out somewhere between a bark and a quack.

For about half a second Elizabeth had to fight the urge to just step into Todd's arms. It had been such a long, strange, painful summer. She'd tried to tell herself that she was coping reasonably well with the death of her close friend Olivia Davidson and the loss of her home. But Todd's presence suddenly made her want to reach out for him and hold him. She could cry and tell him all the things that had gone so wrong, knowing he'd comfort her just like he always had. He might not understand everything exactly, but he would listen and whisper reassurances in her ear. Then he'd kiss her. . . .

*Focus, Elizabeth. Pull it together.* "How was your summer?" she asked. *Great question! What's your favorite color? When is your birthday?* This was Todd, not some stranger.

He shrugged. "Pretty good . . . I missed you." She saw the question in his eyes. He was clearly giving her a way back into *them, us, we.*

"I . . ." She could murmur that she missed him too, take his hand, touch his cheek. They could go to dinner one night, a movie the next. Within weeks they could be ToddandElizabeth. ElizabethandTodd. "I . . . it's nice to see you."

There. The decision had been made. Elizabeth would not take the safe, well-traveled road into

11

her senior year. She would remain on her own—independent, determined. Lonely. But with a million possibilities ahead of her.

"Liz!" It was Jessica, shouting from the end of the long lunch line. "Get your butt over here!"

Elizabeth smiled at Todd. "I'll see you around."

"Yeah . . . see you around." Some of the light had gone out of Todd's brown eyes, but Elizabeth felt a rush of exhilaration as she realized that her freedom was complete.

*Hello, senior year. Hello, life.*

# Jessica Wakefield

About a month after the earthquake, in an attempt to get our minds off our troubles, my dad took me and Elizabeth and our older brother, Steven, to the San Diego Zoo. Go figure. Parents are so lamebrained sometimes, in spite of their good intentions. So we trudged around in the hot sun, eating ice cream and pretending to enjoy ourselves. (I know I'm supposed to be the actress in the family, but Elizabeth's performance that day was worthy of an Academy Award. Steven, of course, was pulling the "I'm in college so this is way too unexistential for me" routine.)

Anyway, I spent about an hour in front of

the tiger's cage — sorry, I mean habitat —
watching this strong, resourceful animal
carrying out a complicated ritual. He'd jump
over a little ravine, stalk through the wooded
area, and go around a tree and then down to
the front of his cage, where he'd pad back to
the ravine and pause for exactly thirty seconds
and leap over it again. He did this about a
hundred times in a row with such concentration
you know he believed the fate of the world
depended on it. He didn't seem to register that
his every meal was provided for, that he had
absolutely no place to go and no control over
his existence.

This, I realized later, is my dad in the
Fowlers' house.

Exactly one day after the earthquake, the

day we went back to try to collect what stuff we could, I passed the door to what had been my dad's study and saw him sitting there, believing, I'm sure, that he was alone. He was surrounded by all his books and pictures, many of them destroyed, and he was weeping. I don't mean like the errant tear of a proud papa at his kid's graduation or something. I mean he was sobbing — his head bowed, his chest heaving, his shoulders shaking.

I'd never seen that before, and I hope never to have to see it again.

Ever since that day my dad has been working insane hours at the law firm. He's been spending any free time dealing with architects and fighting with city planners over the construction of our new house. He even drags my mom on bizarre day trips — like to Disneyland and wine country — just to keep himself busy.

Elizabeth keeps bugging me about "dealing with my pain" from the earthquake. But I'm afraid I can't participate in her group-therapy sessions. I guess ultimately I'm more like my dad than I ever thought. I believe in distraction. As a coping method, it's totally underrated.

You can't control fate. You do what you have to do to get through the day.

# From the Gut

"I hear Mr. Quigley is a total jerk," Enid Rollins said unhappily. "One time he made a girl go sit in the hall because she put a period outside of a set of quotation marks in one of her stories." She pulled out the pencil that had been holding her curly auburn hair in a bun and started chewing on it.

Elizabeth opened the door of the classroom. "All I know is that Sadie Harris wrote her first short story in Mr. Quigley's class and now she's had two books published."

Seventh period, creative writing. Elizabeth had waited for three years to take this elective. As far as she was concerned, this class was her chance. She had been writing poems, stories, and novellas since she was old enough to know that *C-A-T* spelled cat. But she'd never really shared her fiction writing with anyone. Sure, she'd had tons of nonfiction articles published in the school paper, but fiction was different. Fiction required baring the soul. Elizabeth had never had the guts.

Elizabeth slipped into a front-and-center desk, once again struck by how many unfamiliar people populated these familiar spaces. She tried to blot out a feeling of resentment toward the El Carro horde before it fully expressed itself in her mind. *We have it so much easier than they do,* she scolded herself. *But why are there so many of them?* the traitorous voice demanded. *And do they have to look so sullen?*

Elizabeth signed the inevitable seating chart and passed it along, tuning out Enid's paranoid monologue on why she—a right brain—shouldn't be in this left-brain class.

"Let me tell you what this class *isn't* about," Mr. Quigley said, his voice instantly quieting the chaotic buzz of a too-crowded classroom. He was one of those men whose voice and demeanor demanded respect even if he did have mischievous blue eyes, well-defined laugh lines, and a graying ponytail. "It's not about writing saccharine, rhyming love poems about your boyfriends and/or girlfriends." He turned to the chalkboard and wrote No Cheesy Love Poems in huge block letters. "It's not about working out your teen angst on college-ruled notebook paper."

A shiver of fear shot up Elizabeth's spine. She wrote love poems all the time. What did teenagers have to write about *but* teen angst?

*I'm a good writer. I shouldn't be worrying,*

18

Elizabeth assured herself. *I was born to be a writer. Everyone says so.* . . . Suddenly Elizabeth was aware that the classroom was completely silent. And everyone was looking at her.

"Ms. Wakefield?" Mr. Quigley asked again, staring at her. "Can you share with the class why it is you've chosen to take this course?"

Speaking in class. *This* was something she was good at. She'd hardly considered her words before she began. "I've written my whole life," Elizabeth said, the anxiety falling away. "But I need direction. I believe that writing, like everything worthwhile in life, requires dedication and discipline."

*"Please."* It had come from the back of the room. "That's bull."

What? Was he talking to *her?* Elizabeth whipped around in her chair. Mr. Quigley and virtually everyone else in the class were looking toward the back of the room. She knew immediately who had said the words. Brown hair, narrowed green eyes, a shadow of razor stubble, and the kind of smug smile that announced to the world at large that a class-A jerk was present.

Mr. Quigley glanced at the seating chart, which had made its way back to his desk sometime during Elizabeth's little speech. "Conner McDermott," he read. "Enlighten us."

"Writing comes from the gut," Conner said.

"Authors are born, not made." He flicked his eyes toward Elizabeth as if she were a gnat resting on his pastrami sandwich. "*She* probably writes flowery prose about how getting her first zit was a rite of passage."

A few El Carro kids snickered, and Elizabeth drew in a sharp breath. Who was this guy? Why was he attacking her like this? What gave him the right to come into *her* school and make fun of her?

Mr. Quigley raised his eyebrows. "Controversy. I like it."

And that was it—no rebuke, no admonishment, no lecture on peer support. Elizabeth slid a little lower in her seat, battling shock, anger, and rising insecurity. Had she really sounded like a sap? She glanced down at her yellow dress and her low-heeled sandals, feeling uncharacteristically self-conscious. She tucked a strand of pale hair behind her ear. Were all of these new people perceiving her as a total lightweight? Did you have to wear ancient Dr. Martens boots and a tattered black T-shirt in order to be considered artistic?

She wished she'd been able to come up with a scathing response. She wished Enid would stop throwing her round-eyed looks of sympathy. This jerk in the back of the room didn't know her, and he had no right to pass judgment on her. But the class had moved on, and Elizabeth was left with nothing but unvented fury.

She wouldn't forget this. She couldn't. She'd show Conner McDermott and Mr. Quigley that she was made up of more than hearts and sunshine.

Melissa stood in the back of the gym with two of her best friends, Cherie Reese and Gina Cho. She wore her cheerleading sweater, even though the air was warm and heavy, over a white T-shirt and a pair of black bicycle shorts. It somehow made her feel better to be wearing El Carro colors, even if El Carro High was no more than a half acre of rubble at the moment.

"I think that one's Jessica Wakefield," Cherie said, motioning not very subtly through a crowd of fairly ordinary-looking girls to one with long brown hair, a black cat suit, and enough attitude to fill the room.

Melissa shook her head. "I heard she's blond. Besides, that one doesn't look very well coordinated."

Gina clasped her hands and stretched her arms out in front of her. "I hear Jessica has an identical twin sister. Not a cheerleader, though."

Melissa nodded absently, scanning the front entrance for signs of the football team. She predicted they'd be sharing the gym for warm-ups before heading out to the field. She knew she'd be meeting Will at five-thirty in the parking lot, but suddenly that seemed like a long way off.

Her sister was always giving her bits of advice about not depending on Will so intensely, but Lara didn't really understand their relationship. Will was so much more than Melissa's high-school boyfriend, her date to big social events. Will knew her in a way that few other people did. To him she wasn't just Melissa-the-zitproof. He'd known her when she was in eighth grade, the year of the problems, and he'd stood by her. He understood the things she needed to avoid. They never even had to talk about it.

Suddenly a tall blond girl walked through the doors, and Melissa knew instantly it was the famous Jessica Wakefield. She was beautiful, certainly. Melissa had expected that. Jessica had the kind of stereotypical good looks that made guys turn around in the hallways. But the girl was also strong, confident, and . . . intense. Intensity was something Melissa always recognized in a person.

"That's her," she murmured to Cherie and Gina.

"Gotta be," Cherie agreed, twisting her shoulder-length red hair into a scrunchie.

Jessica sauntered into the middle of the group and clapped, as though inviting the earth to resume its rotation now that she'd arrived. "Coach Laufeld will check in at four, so let's stretch and warm up before learning the tryout cheers."

Melissa found herself hanging back as the group came together. She knew she was as fit and limber as any girl in the room. She knew she was the most accomplished gymnast of the group— after twelve years of intensive daily training she would be pitiful if she weren't. She didn't need to show them today how effortlessly she could turn a back flip or how high her jumps soared. There would be time.

Instead she looked again at the doors, tuning her ears to sounds of male banter.

Her sister cautioned her not to depend on Will because she didn't believe Will was dependable. But there Lara was wrong. Melissa could trust Will. She'd never had any reason not to.


"I can't believe you picked our hardest cheer for tryouts, Jess," Amy said, holding her long, blond hair off her neck as she fanned herself. "Half the El Carro girls were tripping over themselves."

"They're all still hanging in the locker room, probably bitching about you," Lila added.

Jessica held open the lobby door for Amy, Lila, and Annie Whitman. "Do you think it was too much?" she asked as she pulled her backpack onto her shoulder. "I just figured I might as well show them what they're in for. We did go to nationals last year."

Amy laughed. "I guess," she said. "Weed the graceless out early."

"If I didn't know better, I'd think you were trying to weed *me* out," Lila said, shaking her right hand. "I think I killed my wrist."

"A few of them were good, though, weren't they?" Annie asked, stopping at the top of the steps. "I mean, what if some of us don't make it?"

Jessica smiled. Annie was one of the most accomplished self-doubters in the world. "You'll make it," Jessica said. "We'll all make it." She glanced down and grabbed Amy's wrist to check her watch. "Damn. I'm late. I'll catch you guys later, okay?"

"We were gonna hang at my house tonight," Amy said. "Why don't you come over after your shift?"

"Can't," Jessica answered. "I wouldn't get there till ten." *And I should probably do my history homework,* she added silently. No need to fill her friends in on her new responsible tendencies.

"C'mon, Jess," Annie said, tucking her short brown hair under her blue baseball cap. "I know you've already figured out who you think will make the squad. I'm gonna need an ego boost."

"And I'm gonna need to get away from your sister," Lila said with a smirk.

Jessica laughed. "Okay. Ten o'clock for half an hour. Then we all need to rest up anyway," she said. "Later!" Jessica walked off quickly, heading for the far end of the parking lot. The one problem with always being fashionably late for school was always getting the worst parking space.

Five twenty-six. Her shift at Healthy started at five-thirty. She hadn't expected practice to go nearly so long. Even though Jessica had told Annie everything was going to be fine, something about practice had bothered her. She'd had a good workout. She hadn't lost a step over the summer. Coach Laufeld seemed to take it for granted that she'd be captain again this year. It wasn't anything like that.

She pictured the cluster of El Carro girls, and then something took shape. It took the shape of a slim girl with thick, dark chestnut hair. If Jessica had heard her name, she couldn't remember it now.

The girl had hardly said a word, and she'd followed the exercises dutifully. She wasn't wearing much makeup or flashy clothes. In spite of the heat and general sweatiness of the gym, she wore a tired black-and-orange cheerleading sweater with the word *Captain* spelled out over her heart in stitched cursive. It was so pathetic that Jessica hadn't felt the least bit threatened—in fact, she'd almost felt sorry for her. But the more Jessica looked at the girl, the more she was struck by her unusual physical grace. She was pale, and her features were delicate. And although she wasn't particularly muscular or powerful looking, she moved with striking precision and intensity.

But the thing that stuck in Jessica's mind was the girl's eyes. They were huge—a sharp, clear light blue, almost like ice. Most disturbing was the way they followed Jessica, barely blinking, for nearly an hour and a half.

Twenty feet from her car, Jessica looked up and stopped dead. It was the guy from her history class. The one she'd been praying she'd run into all afternoon. He was leaning against the cab of an oldish Chevy Blazer, looking damp from a recent shower. So he was an athlete—that much was confirmed. He was parked two spaces from hers. The place was deserted otherwise; there was no way he could fail to notice her.

"Hi," she said brightly as she fished in her bag for the keys to the Jeep.

He looked surprised. "Hi." He didn't smile in return, exactly. His expression was hard to read. He glanced at his watch.

She strode over to him, undaunted, and stuck out her hand. "I'm Jessica Wakefield. You're in my American history class," she told him.

He shook her hand. "I'm Will Simmons." His eyes were guarded, but she felt certain she saw a flash of interest there. Will Simmons. Will . . . where had she heard that name? In a flash it hit her. Will Simmons, all-county quarterback of the El Carro Tigers. Jessica sure knew how to pick 'em.

"Listen," she charged on, mildly amazed at her own boldness, "Crowley is famous for his pop quizzes, and he tests everything he covers in class." She dug a pad of paper and a pen out of her bag. "I'll give you my number in case you ever want to share notes." She jotted down Lila's number and tore out the piece of paper. She pressed it into his hand and walked to the Jeep without another word.

Jessica revved the Jeep and pulled out of the parking lot. She didn't need to look back to know his eyes hadn't left her.

*Ben & Jerry's mint Oreo ice cream . . . homemade blondies with pecans . . . chocolate-glazed crullers.* Elizabeth was hungry. She'd finished her calculus problems and her reading for English, and as she sat staring at her empty creative writing notebook, all she could think about was food.

The problem was, she hadn't eaten enough for dinner. Every time she sat down in a straight-backed upholstered chair in the Fowlers' vast dining room, her stomach tied itself in a knot.

The conversation was awkward. The Fowlers and the Wakefields really didn't have much in common, so her mother filled up the spaces by blathering. It made Elizabeth cringe to see her intelligent mother babbling endlessly without actually saying anything. She hated to imagine what Mr. and Mrs. Fowler thought of her.

Then, as the meal drew to a close, Elizabeth's stomach would twist into a double knot in anticipation of the politically infused conversations between her father and Mr. Fowler. Every night it started as a normal discussion of the events of the day, and every night it deteriorated into an argument over welfare or tax reform or the defense fund. Why couldn't they just talk about the weather?

And it didn't help that Jessica, the single busiest girl on the planet these days, was *never* there to help ease the tension. She was the one member of the family who really knew the Fowlers.

Elizabeth threw her notebook on the bed, then stepped quietly out of her room and down a long corridor. She wished the kitchen weren't so far away. She tiptoed down the grand circular staircase and through the series of rooms that led into the kitchen at the back of the house.

It was weird. Elizabeth had practically spent her life in the Wakefields' kitchen. She often did her homework at the table and loitered around, eating snacks, while she talked on the phone or hung out with her sister or her mom. At the Fowlers' house nobody hung out in the kitchen. Elizabeth frankly doubted Lila had been in there for months. When Lila wanted a diet Coke, she buzzed for it, and a servant whisked it to wherever she was.

Elizabeth paused at the door to the kitchen. *Please, for once be empty,* she begged of the room. She stopped breathing as she pushed gently on the swinging door. Her heart sank. Mrs. Pervis and Elena, the Fowlers' two maids, were there, chatting. She could tell they weren't overjoyed to see her.

"Hello, Jessica," Mrs. Pervis said.

"Hi. It's . . . um, Elizabeth," she corrected. "I was just wondering if I could . . . you know . . . get a snack."

Mrs. Pervis obviously didn't believe in snacking. "Let me get it for you." It sounded more like an order than an offer.

*No, I'll get it myself!* Elizabeth wanted to scream. "Oh. Okay, thanks," she said.

"Would you like some roast beef from dinner? Can I fix you a salad?"

Why couldn't Elizabeth just say she wanted half a pint of Ben & Jerry's? She knew there was some in the freezer. She probably would have had the courage to ask Elena for it, but Mrs. Pervis was just too scary. With one glance she could make

Elizabeth feel more like a cockroach than someone who had been invited to stay. "I—I . . . maybe I'll just have a glass of milk."

Mrs. Pervis stared at her as though she were a six-year-old. "Milk?"

"Or water," Elizabeth quickly amended. "Water would be fine."

Mrs. Pervis nodded tersely and poured a tall crystal glass full of Perrier. "Here you are."

"Thank you," Elizabeth said. She walked back upstairs, feeling like she was going to cry.

When she got to her room, she saw a pile of laundry neatly folded at the foot of the bed. She put the glass down and nearly pounced on it, hoping to find her favorite pair of shorts that had disappeared a day or two ago. No luck. She'd already grilled Jessica on their whereabouts that morning. They had to be in Lila's room.

If her shorts had disappeared into the vast catacombs of Lila's closets, she'd never find them again. But if they'd just been laundered in the last day, they were probably sitting on Lila's bed right now. There was still a chance Elizabeth could get them back, and Lila was over at Amy's with Jessica.

Elizabeth walked to Lila's room and slipped inside. She would just find her shorts and be out of there, no problem, she told herself. She quickly checked the pile on the bed and came up empty-handed. Fighting feelings of discomfort, Elizabeth eased open the third drawer of Lila's dresser. She knew Lila wouldn't be psyched that Elizabeth was going through her stuff, so she tried to search without rumpling anything. Okay, maybe the next drawer. Not there either. Why did Lila have to have so many drawers?

"Elizabeth!"

Elizabeth turned at the sound of the high-pitched squawk. It was Lila, of course.

"Listen, Liz, if you want to borrow my clothes, you could just ask."

Elizabeth's cheeks turned purple. She backed away from the bureau. "But I was just . . . I . . ."

Lila's face was practically twitching with indignation. "I've got a lot to do, okay, so do you mind?" She gestured at the door.

Elizabeth left. There was no point in trying to explain anything. She and Lila weren't friends, and they didn't give each other the benefit of the doubt.

Elizabeth wasn't surprised when the door slammed behind her. She tried to take deep breaths as she padded down the hall.

"Night, Jessica," Mr. Fowler said pleasantly as he passed her on his way to his upstairs study. He hadn't taken his eyes off the papers he was carrying.

"Night," she mumbled in response. Why bother to correct him?

When she got back to her room, she closed the door behind her. The sweaty glass of Perrier had made a ring on the surface of the antique cherry desk Mrs. Pervis had polished that afternoon. She picked up the glass, marched to the bathroom, and dumped its fizzy contents down the toilet.

She hated that stuff.

# Will Simmons

I can't stop thinking about Jessica Wakefield. I've spent too many hours picturing the way her soft-looking hair kept brushing her cheek in history class and remembering her smell (sort of like watermelon and roses mixed together) when she pressed her phone number into my hand in the school parking lot. I've played over and over again in my mind every second I've spent in her presence. I've had thoughts about her that I'm not going to relate here.

It's not just that I'm a horny seventeen-year-old male and she's a beautiful girl, although I don't necessarily expect you to believe me.

There's something about her. She seems _free_, I guess. Spontaneous. She's so confident and uncomplicated compared to . . . well, anyway. And then there's Jessica's body. The way her legs looked in those white shorts . . . Okay, I'll stop.

But I love Melissa. I really, really do. I'm committed to her in a way my friends can't even begin to understand. Sometimes I think I know her better than anyone else, and knowing her like that makes me feel . . . kind of _responsible_ for her. That day in eighth grade when she—well, I can't really go into the details. But the fact is, that day I promised her I would never leave her, and I meant it. I keep my promises.

Melissa needs me. When I imagine my future, I imagine it with her. We'll get married someday. We'll have kids together.

My mom gets on my back about being so serious about a girl while I'm so young. And there's one thing she says that makes some sense. She says I'd better sow a few wild oats now or I could face a real crisis when I'm older and have a family. I mean, Melissa and I aren't married yet. . . .

I gotta stop thinking like this. I can't fool around behind Melissa's back. Especially not with Jessica Wakefield, the girl who's going to take the job of head cheerleader away from her. That would be sick. I couldn't do that to her.

So why haven't I thrown away Jessica's number?

# CHAPTER 3
## Scorn and Bile

"The *Oracle* has always been an award-winning high-school newspaper," Elizabeth said to the group assembled in front of her. "And this year, with the addition of all of you journalists from El Carro, I believe the paper will be better than ever."

*Why am I always compelled to say the right thing?* she asked herself. *Why am I the self-appointed booster for school unity?* So far, El Carro was synonymous with an obnoxious guy in her writing class.

She scanned the crowd. Okay, it wasn't a *crowd*, exactly. Most students weren't frothing at the mouth to spend a sunny afternoon listening to a lecture about editorial integrity and the need for more advertisers. But there were at least fifteen people sitting around the *Oracle* office, making more or less of an attempt to pay attention to what she was saying.

She consulted her clipboard. "Will anyone volunteer to be circulation manager?" she asked hopefully.

Every year that particular question was met with dead silence. Circulation manager was a thankless job. No one wanted to be in charge of picking up the newspaper copies from the printer and then lugging several heavy boxes to school.

A tall girl who was sitting in the front row raised her hand. "I'll do it," she said, her voice barely a whisper.

Major sigh of relief. "Thank you." Elizabeth would have given the girl a hug if she didn't look so totally panic-stricken. "What's your name?"

"Megan Sandborn." Again her voice was little more than a whisper. "I'm a sophomore."

"Oh, well, you need to drive for this job," Elizabeth said.

"That's okay. It's only once a week, right?" Megan said timidly. Elizabeth nodded. "Then my older brother can help me."

"Perfect." Elizabeth smiled at Megan, feeling an immediate connection. Observing the girl's long, strawberry blond ponytail, her neatly buttoned, pinstripe blouse, and the eager way she sat on the front of her seat, Elizabeth was reminded of herself two years before.

"We'll all help you with circulation," Elizabeth promised. "I'll make sure you don't drown under a sea of newspaper."

"So who wants to take charge of getting new advertis—" Elizabeth stopped midsentence as the classroom door banged open. Lila appeared, breathless but perfectly groomed.

Elizabeth felt her stomach twisting. She was half afraid Lila had come to accuse her of stealing clothes in front of the entire newspaper staff.

"Sorry I'm late, Liz." Lila hoisted herself onto a counter, narrowly missing one of the *Oracle*'s expensive layout boards. "I just came from a meeting with my guidance counselor."

Elizabeth set down her clipboard. "What are you doing here?"

"Well, I had a brainstorm. Don't you think the *Oracle* could use a fashion editor?" Lila smoothed her obscenely short miniskirt and flashed Elizabeth a proud smile.

Elizabeth realized her shoulders were hunched up around her ears, and she tried to relax them. Apparently Lila had either forgiven or forgotten the events of the previous night. "A fashion editor?" she repeated slowly.

"Yeah," Lila said buoyantly. "I think I would be perfect for the job, and Mr. Rossetti was just telling me that I need more extracurricular activities."

*No.* The word was in Elizabeth's mind before she'd even thought through the possibility. Maybe Lila's parents had been generous enough to give Elizabeth and her family a place to stay, but that didn't change the fact that Lila took every opportunity to indirectly remind Elizabeth of how much she hated having her around. And the feeling was mutual. The thought of seeing Lila at every *Oracle* meeting . . . it just wouldn't work. They'd probably kill each other. Besides, Lila couldn't commit to a toenail polish color, much less take the time to write an entire article.

The room was silent. Elizabeth could feel her friend Maria Slater's eyes boring into her. Maria liked and respected Lila about as much as Elizabeth did.

"So what do you think?" Lila pressed.

"To be honest, I really don't think the *Oracle* needs—or even has space—for another editor. And even though I'm the editor in chief, I can't just create positions." Elizabeth let out her breath. "Sorry. Students who aren't on the staff can still submit articles for consideration—"

"Random article submissions aren't going to impress anybody on my applications, Liz," Lila snapped.

"Well, that's the only thing I can offer you, Lila," Elizabeth said, trying to maintain her cool. "So, anyway, don't feel like you have to hang out here for the rest of the meeting if you've got stuff to do."

Lila's expression clouded. "I think I'll stay."

"Fine," Elizabeth said tightly. "Stay."

She turned her attention to the rest of the staff. "All right, you guys. Wendy Chen, one of our assistant editors, is going to take you on a quick tour of the office while Maria and I discuss layout and scheduling for the first issue."

Wendy took charge of the room, and Maria got up from her seat.

"Tell me you have a strategy," Maria whispered.

Elizabeth glanced over Maria's shoulder to make sure that Lila had joined the group at the light boards. "Once Lila's been forced to sit through a half-hour open discussion about the relative merits of two-page versus three-page sports layouts, I doubt she'll want to stick around," Elizabeth said under her breath.

Maria smiled and took Elizabeth's clipboard, scanning her notes for the meeting.

"Maybe you should also drag out the boring conversation about new advertisers and fund-raising for as long as possible," she said, grinning.

"By five o'clock Lila will be so bored, she'll join the chess club before agreeing to do any real work for the *Oracle*," Elizabeth predicted.

"Good plan." Maria swept her palm across Elizabeth's before she crossed the room to join Wendy.

Elizabeth sat back, suddenly feeling a wave of exhaustion. She got enough of Lila at "home." School was the one place where she could escape—where Lila was just another of a thousand faces. She'd have to quit the *Oracle* herself before she hired Lila.

\*　　\*　　\*

Jessica was making a mad dash for the Jeep, cursing her platform sandals as she ran. She had stayed after school to talk about uniforms with Coach Laufeld. Now she was almost half an hour late to meet Lila, Amy Sutton, and a bunch of other friends for a Mochaccino and gossip session at House of Java. Lila was going to kill her. Jessica had blown off her best friend too many times this week.

Suddenly Jessica pulled up short. Her heart was pounding harder than ever, but it wasn't from running. Will Simmons's Chevy Blazer was parked next to her Jeep. Today it couldn't be a coincidence. She continued on slowly. *Sweet Valley High parking lot number 4 is fast becoming the most romantic spot on earth.*

He was there. She caught a glimpse of him around the passenger side, retrieving his duffel bag from the backseat. He'd probably just pulled in minutes before. She knew the football team had weight training this afternoon. If she walked roughly the pace of her great-grandmother, they would pass each other.

She looked down, pretending to root for her keys. Today she would keep her mouth shut.

"Jessica."

She'd never loved the sound of her name so much. She looked up. "Will, hi," she said, her voice surprised. Giving him a quick smile, she swung

41

her bag over her shoulder, keys in hand, and pro-
ceeded to the Jeep's driver's-side door.

*Hooking a Guy, Lesson #32: When approaching your target,
it is important to appear indifferent. Always maintain an attitude
of being in a hurry, whether or not that is the case.*

He'd stopped. He was watching her.

Good old #32. Worked every time. And it was
convenient too, considering her entire life ran at
least twenty minutes behind everybody else's.

"You're in a rush." He flattened out the last syl-
lable, not letting it curl into a question.

"Yeah." She threw him an apologetic smile.

*Lesson #12: Be mysterious. Don't offer more information
than is strictly necessary.*

"Crowley's giving the first quiz on Friday." Will
cleared his throat. "Maybe I could take you up on
that offer of exchanging notes."

Jessica turned to face him. His eyes were warm
and friendly. But the way he kept fidgeting, shift-
ing from one foot to the other, told her he was
ready to take off across the lot like a jackrabbit.

She smiled more warmly, wanting to offer genuine encouragement. "That would be great. I'll be

42

home studying tonight. You could drop by and pick them up. . . ." Had she gone too far?

He hesitated, toying with the handle of his duffel. "Fifty-seven Hillside Drive," she continued, hoping she hadn't scared him off. "It's the big stone one on the right at the top of the hill. It's not actually my permanent home. Our place got flattened by the earthquake, so we moved in with family friends, and we probably won't be moving back home for a few months. . . ." *Okay, Jess,* she counseled herself, *turn off the babble faucet before you drown him.*

She opened the door, climbed into the driver's seat, and stuck the key in the ignition, wondering how long he'd wait to answer.

"Around eight-thirty." It was hardly more than a whisper. She wasn't completely certain she'd even heard him right.

But she rewarded him with a grin in the hope that she had. She threw the Jeep into reverse without saying good-bye.

*Lesson #5: Leave while you're ahead.*

"Sorry, Jess. I'm cutting you off. As of now, the bar's closed."

"But Lizzie! I *need* another Mochaccino!" Jessica whined.

"Are you kidding me?" Elizabeth asked, leaning over the emerald green counter at House of Java and staring into Jessica's eyes. "The caffeine-induced hyperness is coming off you in waves, dear sister."

At that moment Jessica noticed she was tapping a metal spoon against the counter at an alarming staccato pace. She covered the spoon with a clatter and smiled at Elizabeth.

"Okay, maybe you're right," she said with a laugh. "Can I at least have some water? It's antisocial to be without a beverage when all your friends are sipping."

"One water coming up," Elizabeth said, pulling open the glass door of the refrigerator. She placed a bottle of springwater in front of Jessica and wiped her hands on her purple apron. "So what are you guys doing? Planning the cheerleading strategy for the season?" Elizabeth asked, casting a glance in the direction of Jessica's friends. Jessica, Amy, Lila, Annie, and a couple of other girls had pulled together a few of the comfy, upholstered chairs in the back corner near a particularly packed bookshelf.

"Cheerleading isn't our life, Liz," Jessica said. "How do you know we're not studying?"

"Are you?"

"No. We're talking about cheerleading," Jessica chirped.

Elizabeth rolled her eyes and laughed.

"Thanks for the water, Liz!" Jessica said, strolling away.

"Hey! Aren't you going to pay for that?" Elizabeth called. Jessica pretended not to hear her. She'd pay Elizabeth back later. Probably. Well, more like maybe.

"That Cherie girl is really good," Amy said as Jessica plopped into a red velvet chair. "Did you see how quickly she was picking up the moves?"

"Yeah. And what about her friend? Melissa or Melinda, I think her name is?" Annie added, blowing on her coffee. "She was El Carro's captain."

Jessica sighed. "I can't believe she actually wears her cheerleading sweater to practice. I mean, who does she think she is?"

"I don't know, Jess," Jade Wu piped up. "She *is* really good. And how would you feel if SVH had collapsed in the earthquake and suddenly you weren't captain anymore?"

"Yeah. That must suck for her," Annie added.

"In case you guys have forgotten, I'm *not* captain anymore," Jessica reminded them as she twisted open her water bottle. "Coach made it clear that we're all equals here."

"Sure. That's why you're teaching the cheers and running the practices," Lila said. She held up her pinky as she sipped her cappuccino. "You know you've got captain in the bag, Jess."

Jessica couldn't help smiling. She'd love to be

modest, but why deny the truth? Her friends were right. Coach Laufeld wasn't going to demote her. She might make someone her cocaptain, but barring severe debilitating injury, Jessica Wakefield would be captain of the cheerleading squad again this year. No one made captain as a junior and didn't make it again as a senior. But the security of her own position didn't change the fact that her friends were still worried about their spots on the squad.

Jessica put her water down on the table and leaned forward. She picked up Jade's sleek black ponytail and started braiding. "Listen, you guys. I think I know what Laufeld's strategy is going to be for selecting the team."

"Really?" Amy's eyes lit up. "Do you know how many she's taking?"

"Or, more important, how many from each school?" Annie asked.

"That's just it," Jessica said. "Laufeld's big on promoting school unity—you know, pretending there's no difference between us and those El Carro losers. So I don't think she's considering the number of people from each school. I think she's going to pick the strongest cheerleaders, no matter where they're from."

"That's a relief," Jade said.

"So here's what everyone should remember for tryouts," Jessica began. As she reminded her friends of what had won them all their positions in the past, she felt more and more at ease. It had been a long summer, but she was back where she was supposed to be. Her friends needed her. The squad needed her. And it felt good to know that even with all the new competition, not everything had changed.

Jessica was right back on top where she belonged.

Tick. Tick. Tick. Had the library *ever* been this quiet? The tiny sounds emanating from Elizabeth's wristwatch sounded like a bomb about to detonate. Elizabeth liked quiet, but this place had an eerie resemblance to a tomb. Still, it was better than the atmosphere at the Fowlers'—better than listening to Lila play each and every one of her CDs at a volume slightly above that of a nuclear explosion.

She was grateful to have had a shift at House of Java this afternoon, even if Jessica had weaseled three free coffees and a bottle of water out of her. It got her out of dinner, at least. And she was thrilled that school had finally started so she had an excuse to spend evenings in the library. She popped a couple of M&M's in her mouth. Too many dinners at the Fowlers had caused her best-fitting jeans to hang off her hips.

Elizabeth just wished that there were a few more people here. Apparently no one else in Sweet

Valley felt the need to study on the second night of school. Even Elizabeth wasn't studying. She was pondering the stubborn emptiness of her creative-writing notebook.

Elizabeth stared at the one lonely line of text written there.

Due Wednesday: a one-page essay on the subject of loss. Be creative, not maudlin.

She had quoted Mr. Quigley's words directly when she copied down the assignment. Elizabeth opened the dictionary she had brought with her.

**maudlin** 1: Embarrassingly sentimental.

But loss *was* sentimental. What did the man *want* from them? Blood on the page? Elizabeth slammed the dictionary shut. *Loss, boss, moss, toss* . . . No rhymes. Rhymes were maudlin. *L* stands for loss. *O* stands for over. *S* stands for sadness. The other *s* stands for—

Why was she even bothering? This essay was simply not happening tonight. She'd have to get up at dawn and try to get inspired by the sunrise.

Oh, wait. No sunrises. Sunrises were definitely maudlin. Elizabeth pushed her hair away from her face, sighing heavily. She'd finished her calculus.

She'd read a chapter of history. Why couldn't she do this one stupid assignment?

Elizabeth sat up straighter. Someone was watching her. She could feel it. She turned ninety degrees and scanned the reading room.

*Oh.* Her palms prickled. Thirty feet away, hunched over in one of the large, comfortable chairs by the library's bay windows, was none other than Conner McDermott. With the possible exceptions of Jessica and Lila, he was probably the last person she would have expected to see here.

Elizabeth spun back around. Conner's eyes had seemed glued to whatever he'd been holding in his lap, but the guy *had* been watching her. She was sure of it. *Maybe he feels bad about yesterday,* she thought.

Or maybe Conner had been so impressed by Elizabeth's analysis of Jack London's short story "To Build a Fire" in class today, he'd had an epiphany about her intelligence.

Then again, Conner hadn't even seemed to be paying attention. He had kept his head bent over a piece of paper on which Elizabeth had happened to notice he was sketching the girl sitting in front of him, Maisie Greene. Maisie was pretty in a hippie, free-to-be-you-and-me kind of way.

But the fact that Conner was in the library tonight had to mean something. Maybe he was a serious thinker who hadn't had a chance to develop his social skills. Or maybe his rudeness was a symptom of an actual mental illness. Or maybe he was there to pick up chicks. (Probably the way he referred to women.) That would be really annoying. . . .

But doubtful, she realized in a little burst of self-pity. What kind of worthwhile girl would he hope to pick up in the library on the second night of school?

*This is ridiculous.* She was sitting in a nearly empty library, staring at a blank notebook, feeling like a loser, and obsessing about some guy who'd been mean to her. Clearly Elizabeth needed to resolve this. Once she and Conner reintroduced themselves on a seminormal footing, she could forget he existed.

Elizabeth slid her chair away from the table with grim determination. If Conner McDermott was even half as unpleasant as he had been yesterday, she was going to make him wish he'd never opened his mouth. Now that she'd had time to simmer, she wouldn't be afraid to let loose a few barbs of her own.

She stopped in front of Conner and waited for him to look up from his notebook. Why was her heart pounding like this? She could feel tiny droplets of sweat gathering on her upper lip.

Okay, he was *not* going to look up. Not without

provocation. This confrontation wasn't getting off to the positive start she had hoped for.

"Hey," Elizabeth said finally.

Conner flicked his green eyes in her direction. "Hey."

"I'm Elizabeth Wakefield." She fidgeted with the front pocket of her jeans. His gaze was so intense, she felt stripped down to her underwear—flowered underwear that she suddenly felt the need to replace at her first opportunity. "I'm, uh, in your creative-writing class."

*His* creative-writing class? Damn. She should have said that *he* was in *her* class. She had just set up a power dynamic that worked completely in Conner's favor. Not that it mattered.

He nodded and half smiled. "Right—you're the hearts-and-flowers girl."

Her cheeks warmed with anger. His smile didn't make up for his sarcasm. "And you're the scorn-and-bile boy."

"Oooh. Barbie has a brain, huh?" The smile was gone. His voice was low, gravelly.

"Oooh. Ken has an attitude," she snapped back.

Conner smirked (that was the only word for the snarl with a twist that lit his face). "So we're suddenly a couple?" He leaned back in the chair and crossed his arms in front of his chest.

"Excuse me?" Elizabeth said, her blood pressure rising. She was too mad to care that they were in the middle of a library. "Who said anything about a *couple?*"

"You did. Barbie and Ken. Ken and Barbie." He was tapping his pen against his notebook, totally at ease, watching her with amusement in his eyes.

"You know I didn't mean . . . What I said was—" She had reached her boiling point.

"Listen, *Elizabeth.* You saw me, then you worked up your courage to come over and talk to me." He smiled—a real smile this time. "Admit it. You're fishing for a date."

A date? A date? She would kill him. She would take his pen and shove it up his nose. No, she would shove it down his throat. No, she would . . . do something worse. She didn't know what, exactly. But it would be very, very painful.

Elizabeth finally found her voice. "I wouldn't go on a date with you if you were the last guy on earth."

Conner's smile had bloomed into a full-blown grin. "That's usually the line the girl gives the guy right before they ride off into the sunset—"

"Shut up!" Elizabeth yelled.

He shrugged. "No need to get all worked up. I was just stating a simple fact."

She hated him. Elizabeth usually reserved that emotion for Nazis and telemarketers, but in this case she would make an exception. Conner McDermott was hands down the most obnoxious guy on the planet. The most obnoxious *person* on the planet.

52

She would never, ever speak to him again. Without another word Elizabeth turned and strode toward the table where she had left her books.

"Nice chatting with you," Conner called.

*Hate.* That was the word. *Hate.*

Melissa's hand was shaking as she pressed the receiver to her ear, listening to the phone ring. She took one last look at the lined notebook paper she'd found in Will's glove compartment—at the loopy pink handwriting of some random girl. She balled the paper up in a fist. He probably didn't even know she had it.

It took four long rings before someone picked up. "Hello?"

It was a girl's voice, of course. Medium pitched, confident, accustomed to hearing the phone ring, lazy about picking it up.

Melissa took a deep breath to make sure her own voice didn't come out shaky. "Who is this?" She wanted to sound flat, unemotional.

"Lila Fowler," the voice said, rich with indignation. "Who is *this?*"

Melissa paused, pulling at the hem of her blouse. "It doesn't matter."

She hung up the phone and tossed the balled-up paper in the trash can. She gazed at the ink marks bleeding over her sweaty palm.

# Elizabeth Wakefield

## <u>Creative</u> <u>Writing</u>

### <u>Loss</u>

I used to believe that inherent in the word <u>loss</u> was the implication that what is lost can be found. A girl cries over the loss of her dog—then shouts with joy when a neighbor returns him. A mother finds her child's mittens in a department store's overflowing lost-and-found bin. A businessman loses his vast fortune one year, then recovers it the next.

When I was six years old, I found a beautiful shell on the beach—pale, translucent pink, the curvature so delicate and fine, I believed it held magical powers. I kept it in an old cigar box lined with gleaming red silk. I decorated the outside of the box with several of the shell's more ordinary cousins. I only took it out when I needed a special wish granted. One day I went to the box and discovered the shell shattered into a million tiny pieces . . . not much more than a layer of dust to dull the silk. The shell was gone, and it could never be replaced.

This summer I lost another, much more beautiful treasure. Her name was Olivia Davidson, and she was a fiery gem among the colorless stones that make up our world. I wake up every morning, and for the first few seconds of my day everything seems in its place. Then I remember.

Now I understand the true meaning of loss: the recognition, day after day, that the thing you lost can never be found.

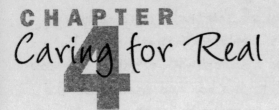

# CHAPTER 4
## Caring for Real

Okay, so maybe she wouldn't ordinarily choose a short black dress and silver sandals for a night with her history books, but Will didn't have to know that.

It was 8:37, and Jessica was pacing the Fowlers' plush family room. She gave the scene a quick once-over. Textbook and notebooks were fanned artfully over the coffee table in easy reaching distance of the plush leather couch. Soft music—Handel's *Water Music*, according to the CD box—played on the entertainment center that sparkled with more lights, buttons, and levers than an air-traffic-control tower. A bowl of popcorn rested on the thick wall-to-wall carpet.

Would they sit on the couch or the floor? *Will I actually get him to sit at all?* Jessica wondered.

Will Simmons was skittish. It couldn't be denied. But somehow it only made him more attractive to her. She was so sick of guys who hid their insecurities behind a fake layer of conceit.

But *why* was he skittish? *Why* was a word

she'd spent very little time with over the past couple of months. It was bad company, as far as she was concerned, only making simple things complicated. And yet she felt compelled at least to try to answer it.

Will wasn't shy. She knew in her heart he wasn't. She ticked off some other possibilities in her mind: He'd been hurt by a girl in the past. He felt traitorous falling right in with a Sweet Valley girl. He found Jessica's style intimidating. Those were all good answers.

The doorbell rang, and Jessica went running for the stairs. She'd beat Eduardo to the door if she had to tackle him. Nothing scared off a guy like being greeted by a butler. Jessica clacked across the marble foyer, skidded to the door, and gave the approaching Eduardo a menacing look. He disappeared, and Jessica threw open the door.

Jessica's heart stopped. Will was really nice to look at. His hair was unruly, and his shirt was coming a little untucked, but it didn't make him any less appealing.

She smiled, suddenly feeling nervous. "This isn't really my house," she reminded him, noticing his look of skeptical awe as he glanced around the ridiculously opulent surroundings.

"Right," he said. He was still standing halfway out the door, his thumbs hooked in the front pockets of his jeans. She had the feeling if she made one false move, he was out of there.

She gave him a friendly smile, hoping to ease the first-date-type tension in the air. *Even though this isn't really a date,* she reminded herself. "My notes and stuff are downstairs. Do you want to come down for a minute? I can gather them up quickly if you're in a rush. . . ."

She hoped he wouldn't accept the offer—that he was here because he wanted to be—not just for her notes. But Will was hard to read. Not like some guys, who couldn't hide their slobber no matter how hard they tried. (He'd soon find out her notes weren't all that good anyway, what with her staring at him so much of the class.)

"So are you?" Jessica asked.

"What?"

"In a rush?" She almost let out a nervous giggle but caught herself in time.

"Oh, no. Not really." He shrugged.

"Cool," Jessica said. She took his hand. It was risky, she knew, but she had a feeling he'd never move out of the doorway if she didn't do something. He didn't pull it away. She held his fingers gently, loosely, using them only to guide him down the stairs. Once she'd gotten him safely into the family room, she dropped his hand, sorry to lose the warmth of his fingers against hers.

Will didn't make a move to sit, so she walked

away from him over to the coffee table and knelt by it, gathering her notes, trying to decide whether or not to call his bluff. Or whether he was really bluffing at all. *Please don't let him just take the notes and leave.*

But before Jessica could gather all the papers together, he was standing over her, holding out his hand. She took it, her heart hammering. She stood to meet him, her chin lifted to hold his gaze. He was so close, she could smell the citrusy soap he used.

His eyes probed hers with jarring intensity. Her head swam as he placed one hand lightly against her cheek. He moved it along her cheekbone to her temple and then her hair.

This wasn't like any first date she'd ever had. No "what's your favorite movie?" No rundown on number of siblings, favorite vacation spots, or major extracurricular activities. In fact, this wasn't much like a date at all. But it was intense and thrilling and wonderful. She'd never felt such intimacy with someone she knew so little.

His gaze moved to his own hand as he touched her hair, her shoulder. His eyes moved down the length of her body before returning to her face. Her cheeks were deeply flushed.

"Jessica, you are so beautiful," he told her in a whisper.

He put one hand on each of her hips and

pulled her closer. Then he bent his head and kissed her.

Her thoughts scattered, regrouped, then scattered again. She sighed as his kiss grew deeper and more urgent. His strong body pressed into hers. She felt the blood pulsing in her head, making her dizzy and faint. Suddenly he was pushing her backward. They fell together onto the leather couch. But even as her body responded, her mind groped to form a word.

*Fast.* The word finally broke through. *Too fast.*

But she didn't want to let go. *It feels so good.*

Will's hand found its way to the zipper at the back of her dress, and it startled her body enough to allow her mind back in charge.

Jessica pulled away and tried to catch her breath. "Don't," she whispered. "We're going too fast." Her face was open with honesty. She wasn't playing games. Inexplicably, she'd started to care about this guy for real now.

He sat up slowly and took a deep breath, his big shoulders hunched. "Okay. You're right. I'm sorry." He was looking right at her.

"Don't be," she said, her heart expanding with happiness. On some level she'd been afraid he'd act the way other guys had—evasive, impatient, annoyed. He was different.

She cuddled in close, circling his waist with her arm. "We've got time," she murmured. "We've got a whole year of days to spend together."

The words were out before she even registered their magnitude. She held her breath. What was she talking about? She barely knew Will! It was against Jessica's code to talk about the future. But for some reason, she found herself *wanting* to trust him.

He stood, straightened his shirt, and scooped up his backpack.

She stood too. For a moment she thought she really had scared him away this time. But then he gave her a tender, lingering kiss before he turned to go.

"You are something, Jessica," he said quietly. "I won't forget."

She let him go, a knot of emotion forming in her throat. *Why does he make it sound so final? Isn't this just the beginning?*

Dear Diary,

So, it took Jessica approximately thirty-six hours to find the love of her life among the men of El Carro. Why am I not surprised?

Jessica meets Mr. Perfection, and I meet Satan-with-a-backpack.

Okay, I'm sounding bitter. Let me recount the story. Jess just came up here and told me that the Blazer that peeled out of here about fifteen minutes ago belonged to Will Simmons—who is, according to Jessica, El Carro's quarterback and Ken's main rival for the first-string position on the team. Jessica says they met yesterday and the sparks flew. She was fiercely attracted to him, and apparently he felt it too because they just cemented their new love by making out downstairs.

Now, normally I would write this off as Jessica doing the diving-without-looking thing she's so famous for, but this time it's different. You should have heard the way she was talking about him. It was like . . . well, she just had this look on her face and this tone that I've never heard before. And Will sounds pretty cool. Nice . . . and straightforward. Not like the self-centered players Jessica usually falls for. The dark, grungy, leather-wearing types who have three other girlfriends and a one-track mind.

Leave it to Jessica to find the single most worthy El Carro-ite in the senior class. (Before the end of the first week of school.) Leave it to me to find the rudest, most offensive one.

This couldn't be happening. This was simply a nightmare. Elizabeth had *thought* that she'd woken up, taken a shower, come to school, and eaten lunch with Enid and Maria out in the courtyard. Even the hour she had spent working in the *Oracle* office had been an illusion. In fact, she was still asleep in her canopy bed at the Fowlers'.

"Your assignment, Ms. Wakefield?" Mr. Quigley repeated for the second time.

"Uh . . . right." Elizabeth swallowed the tennis-ball-size lump that was forming in her throat. This was not a nightmare. This was not a test of the emergency broadcast system. She actually had to hand her assignment to Conner McDermott, who was going to read it aloud to the entire class.

Elizabeth stood up, silently cursing her knees, which were shaking more or less uncontrollably, and walked toward the back of the room. She also had a few, choice, unspoken words for Mr. Quigley, who had decided that everyone in the class had to trade assignments with another student—a student of his choosing, no less. Mr. Quigley was obviously a sick, sick man. He claimed that hearing your work read aloud by an impartial reader could help you objectively identify flaws in your own work. But Conner wasn't exactly impartial. She leaned over and put her one-page paper on Conner's desk.

"Here's mine," Conner said, handing Elizabeth his assignment.

Elizabeth felt her face grow red. This guy was not going to let up. He'd decided that she was a walking, talking mannequin, and he wasn't going to change his opinion. He was the furthest thing from the sympathetic reader she needed. He would hate her piece and probably ridicule it publicly. Elizabeth almost wished there would be another earthquake—one that would open up the floor and swallow her whole. Scratch that—swallow *him* whole.

She yanked the assignment out of Conner's hand, made her way back down the aisle, and sank into her desk chair, slouching as low as she could. No doubt she would hear cackling from the back row at any second now. *Don't let him get to you. That's what he wants.* Elizabeth took a deep breath, then exhaled yoga style. Okay. She was ready.

Elizabeth placed Conner's paper on her desk and leaned over it. Her eyes moved quickly across the page, digesting the words he had written. The first line was passable. Could be luck. She continued to read. The third line. The fourth line. The fifth line. Each was better than the last.

She didn't want to read anymore. She told her mind to shut up, but it said what it was thinking anyway: *He's good. Conner is really, really good.* The language in the assignment was actually funny, but it still conveyed the deeper emotion of the piece. Elizabeth's heart beat a little faster as she raced toward the end of the essay, almost against her will.

She wanted to be angry that Conner was talented. She still wanted to hate him. And she did, of course. Only it was mixing with something else. Respect? *No!* Sympathy? *Too ridiculous.* What, then?

As demented as Conner was, he was obviously human too. He not only felt things deeply, he expressed them deeply.

"Ms. Wakefield, if you would like to reenter the earth's atmosphere and join the rest of the class, you can hear Mr. McDermott read your paper to us."

"Sorry," Elizabeth said quietly. She closed her eyes, bracing herself as Conner ambled to the front of the room.

"'I used to believe that inherent in the word *loss* . . . ,'" Conner began. His voice was serious and smooth. She waited for the twist of sarcasm in his tone, but it didn't come.

As he read, Elizabeth felt the words wash over her. She felt a tiny surge of pride as his voice gave new perspective to her work, but she wrestled it back down. Conner would find a way to mock it. Wait until he got to the part about Olivia. He was probably just pacing the class for his big, cruel finale.

Conner paused before he read the last line. She crossed her arms defensively over her chest. The room was eerily silent.

Conner seemed to be waiting until he had everyone with him. And when he finally read the last bit, he did so with such honesty and sincere empathy that Elizabeth felt she would burst into tears.

Conner was quiet for a moment. No one in the class moved. Finally he strode toward her desk, catching her eye and holding it as he got close. He placed the paper on her desk, apparently giving the cue to the rest of the class to start buzzing again.

"I'm impressed," Mr. Quigley said, and Elizabeth's entire body was suffused with pure pleasure. "Any comments from the class?" A pause. "Conner?"

Elizabeth stopped breathing and froze. She wouldn't turn around to look at him.

"Moving." The word penetrated Elizabeth's heart. "Surprisingly moving."

Elizabeth was having some kind of nervous breakdown. That had to be it. Her hands were shaking, her palms were itching, and her pulse was roaring in her ears. She searched her mind for some clue as to what was happening to her. *Moving . . . surprisingly moving.* Why did his words suddenly mean so much to her?

She looked back down at his essay, finally allowing her eyes to travel to the bottom of the page. She squinted at the cramped scrawl at the bottom and almost laughed out loud. He'd signed it "Bile Boy."

She looked over her shoulder at Conner and found his eyes. He actually smiled. And Elizabeth found herself smiling back.

# Conner McDermott
## <u>Creative Writing</u>

### <u>Loss</u>

My first experience with loss came along when my bike was still a four-wheeler and I was the neighborhood spitball target. The guy with the perpetual gapped teeth and bad hair. The one whose mother dressed him just this side of feminine because she always wanted a girl. I was a bullys dream.

But there was one thing I had over everyone else. One claim to fame that gave me this slight advantage over the rest. I had the greatest collection of baseball cards in the history of William Walters Grade School. Everyone envied it. And no one stood a chance of trading up in this world if he couldn't trade with me.

The most impressive card I had—the one every kid in the neighborhood came by to view at least once a month—was a Roger Maris rookie card, signed by the legend himself. It had been given to me by my father in a rare show of parental affection. I had been warned to take good care of it. There were only so many treasures in this life, and this was one of them.

The day after my dad walked out on

us, Ricky Ramirez, the most evil guy on my block, got his brothers to distract me while he broke into my room and took my card. When his lackeys let me go, I ran straight to my stash and knew instantly that it was gone. Hours later I was still lying on my floor, covered in baseball cards and staring at my ceiling, when Ricky's little sister, Tia, walked into my room. She told me Ricky had buried it somewhere in her backyard, but he wouldn't tell her where.

We dug up the whole place, she and I. Dug until our fingernails were gone. I had never even spoken to this girl before, but she stayed out there with me, skipping dinner, skipping dessert, digging until it was dark. We never found it.

It wasn't until about ten years later, when I was listening to Tia give a blow-by-blow of one of her parents' legendary fights and subsequent make-out marathons, that it hit me. If I hadn't lost that card, I would never have met my best friend.

My father was right. There are few treasures in this life, and that useless piece of cardboard helped me find one.

# CHAPTER 5
## An Identifiable Enemy

Whoever decided that gym class should take place in the middle of the day obviously had a cruel, sick sense of humor. Jessica brushed her hair back from her face and fanned at her cheeks, then studied her complexion in the locker-room mirror. No good. She was still all blotchy.

"Li?" she called. "I'll meet you in class. I left my compact in my locker."

"Okay. I'll be there as soon as I find a bag for my head," Lila said. "Remind me never to let Amy talk me into racing again. I wasn't made to perspire."

"You're just bitter from eating my dust," Amy said, throwing her dirty T-shirt at Lila.

Jessica left the locker room to the sound of Lila's disgusted squeal. "Later!" she called, not expecting an answer. She glanced at the clock above the SVH trophy wall. Five minutes to haul her butt across the school and back, which would probably just make her face blotch worse. Oh, well. It was worth a shot.

Jessica hurried around the corner and slammed right into a brick wall . . . a very pleasantly scented brick wall. Her heartbeat sped up.

"Slow down, Jessica," Will said, putting his hands on her shoulders. The sensation of his fingertips on her skin was almost more than she could take.

"Hi," she said, wondering what to do with her eyes. Just being in his presence after last night made her blush. Then she noticed the smile. She wasn't sure she'd actually seen one on his face before. It was a fugitive smile, though—one he would have kept down if he could have. "You're happy," she said.

He quickly removed his hands from her shoulders, stuffed them into his pockets, and looked around.

"I am," Will said quietly. "I'm enjoying one of the better half hours of my life."

Jessica's heart rate skyrocketed. She could tell that part of his happiness stemmed from seeing her, but there was something else behind it as well. "What's up?"

"I really shouldn't be . . ."

Jessica touched his arm, tilting her face toward his. "Tell me."

After a long look at her face he sighed. "I just got out of a meeting with Coach Riley," Will said, glancing over his shoulder. "Ken Matthews quit the team. I'm going to start as quarterback."

"Oh, Will! You must be so psyched. Congratulations!" On impulse she wrapped her arms around his neck and held him close.

Will gave her a quick squeeze in return, then pulled away.

Jessica's arms fell to her sides and she swallowed hard, trying to keep the confusion from her eyes. Why was he shrugging her off?

"Sorry. I mean . . . I shouldn't have said anything yet. It's supposed to be a big secret. I better go."

She would have been hurt. She probably would have been angry. But moments after rushing away from her, he paused a few yards down the hall, turned back, and gave her such an intense look that she felt her heart step out of its even rhythm. She'd capture that look in her memory like a snapshot.

"I'll call you," he said.

"Right. So, I'll talk to you later," she murmured to his retreating back, more to make sure her voice still worked than to keep up any communication.

She started when the bell rang. "Damn." There was no point in going to her locker now. It was too late, and no amount of powder could cover the redness in her cheeks.

Will was going to call her! Maybe later they would celebrate. As Jessica watched the girls pour out of the locker room, her imagination shifted into overdrive. Will Simmons was the starting quarterback. That made him a local celebrity. She would undoubtedly be captain of the cheerleading squad. It was almost too much. Too perfect. Suddenly she felt like fate had played a miraculous hand in bringing them together.

She might even ask him to go with her to the dance on Saturday.

She smiled happily. It had been so long since she'd been part of an actual couple, she could barely remember what it felt like. But she hoped that was where she and Will were headed. She was tired of dating around. Tired of finding out that every guy was just like the last. But Will really was different. After an awful summer, her senior year was spreading itself before her in a rosy glow of social ascendancy and romantic contentment. It would start at the school dance on Saturday night and get better from there.

It was almost too good to be true.

Melissa spotted Lila Fowler in the mirror of the bathroom, checking the lines of her freshly lipsticked mouth. As much as she'd dreaded this moment, Melissa was now ready for action.

It hadn't taken Melissa long to figure out who Lila was. She'd already taken notice of Lila at cheerleading practice; she just hadn't put the name to the face. And now that she'd had a moment to study the girl, she was relieved to see that although Lila was very pretty, she was not Will's type at all. She was too dressed up, too made-up, too prissy. Will couldn't stand the snotty-rich-girl type. His family had too many money problems for him to tolerate that kind of attitude.

Melissa felt confident that whatever was going on with this girl was entirely one-sided. It always was. Will was an exceptional guy. He was amazing looking, a star athlete, and well liked by just about everyone. Of course girls were always throwing themselves at him. It was natural. *So why didn't he just throw away her number?* an annoying voice in her head wanted to know.

"You're Lila Fowler, right?" Melissa didn't bother to let her answer the question. "I'm Melissa Fox. I think we met at cheerleading."

Lila nodded, her expression skeptical.

Melissa decided to dive right in. "I think you know my boyfriend, Will Simmons."

Lila shook her head. "I don't, actually. I have heard his name, though."

Melissa cleared her throat. "Why did you give him your telephone number if you don't know him?" she asked tonelessly.

Lila's eyes narrowed. "*Excuse* me, but I did not give Will Simmons or any other guy in this school my number," she spat out. "It's not my style. Besides, what makes you think it was me? It's not like I'm the only person at that number."

This threw Melissa. She hadn't considered that the number was given to Will by somebody else. She didn't know Lila, but she was pretty sure the girl wasn't lying. Melissa had a talent for telling when someone wasn't being truthful. Did Lila have a sister?

Melissa had to change her tactics and fast. She smiled apologetically. "Listen, Lila, I'm sorry. I should have guessed that. Things are a little tense with the mixing of schools and all. I just wanted to make sure that this girl, whoever she is, knows the deal." Her smile went from apologetic to self-amused. "But I should have known it wasn't you. You're obviously not a girl who goes begging for dates."

She studied Lila's face carefully. It softened with flattery, just as Melissa predicted.

"Just so you know that I really am sorry," Melissa ventured on, "I was wondering if you would like to join a bunch of us at Secca Lake after practice tonight. It'll be mostly El Carro people. We—the guys in particular—are trying to figure out which Sweet Valley High people are worth hanging out with, if you know what I mean?"

Lila was still skeptical but melting fast. Melissa knew this would work if she kept pushing it.

"Apology accepted," Lila said, almost warmly.

"I've got plans tonight, but maybe I can take a rain check?"

Melissa nodded. "Anytime. My friends would be psyched."

She watched Lila go, feeling her spirits sink. Who had given Will that number? Melissa so much preferred an enemy she knew to one she didn't.

Will took Jessica's hand as he led her to the outdoor seating area of Michael's Café on Wednesday evening. Jessica smiled as they walked out into the warm evening air. The view was spectacular—waves crashing against the shore below and the deep blue Pacific stretching out to meet the horizon. Jessica had never been to this restaurant, but now she knew she'd always remember it as her and Will's place. Their first real date.

"Do you always celebrate forty-five minutes outside of town?" Jessica asked as she slipped into her seat, smoothing the skirt of her black linen dress beneath her.

"I just didn't want to bump into anyone from school," Will said.

"Why not?" Jessica asked as she placed her napkin in her lap. She would have loved bumping into a couple of her friends with Will by her side.

"Well, we're celebrating something no one's

supposed to know about, for one," Will answered. "And I . . . I just wanted to be alone."

Jessica's heart warmed. Good answer. She couldn't exactly fault him for wanting her all to himself. "I get it. There would be nothing better than a crowd of football players to spoil the mood of a first date."

Will's eyes flicked down, and he cleared his throat. He took a deep breath and looked at her for a moment, then focused at a point over her right shoulder. "I wanted to talk to you about that."

"About what?" Jessica asked, picking up a bread stick.

Will cleared his throat again. He fiddled with his fork, then put it down again. He took his water goblet and downed about half the glass. "Jessica, I—"

"Good evening, sir, madam." A young waiter in a crisp white shirt bowed next to their table. "Let me tell you about our specials for the evening. . . ."

The first item on the waiter's list had something to do with squid and lemon. Jessica winced, and Will let out a little snort of laughter. The waiter kept talking, but Jessica glanced up at Will, mortified that he'd caught her unsophisticated reaction. But Will was grinning. And his full-on smile was heart stopping.

The waiter moved on to an equally unappetizing duck dish, and Will stuck his tongue out slightly and crossed his eyes for a split second. Jessica barely even caught it, but it was enough to nearly make her choke on her bread stick. The waiter stopped when he heard her gagging. Jessica reached for her water glass.

"Can I get madam some more water?" the waiter asked.

Jessica nodded. She took a long sip.

"Are you okay?" Will asked through laughter.

Jessica put down her glass. "I'm fine," she said with a grin. "What do you think that guy will do if I order a burger?"

"He'll probably have a heart attack," Will said, still catching his breath from his laughing fit. He looked at Jessica, his eyes shining. They looked even more incredibly blue when he smiled. "I haven't laughed like that in a long time," he said.

"Glad I could be of service," Jessica quipped. "You should laugh like that all the time. The way your face scrunches up is very attractive."

"Oh, thanks," Will said. "And you look lovely when you're choking."

They laughed again, and Jessica took another sip of her water. "So, was there something you wanted to talk to me about?"

Will held her gaze for a long moment, and Jessica saw a cloud of uncertainty pass over his features. He looked down at his watch, then back up at her again, and the smile was back, if not as strong as before.

"It's not important," he said, picking up his menu. "I think we'd better just get ready for the waiter's return." He disappeared behind the menu.

"Sounds like a plan," Jessica said, following suit. As she scanned the list of entrées, she tried to keep herself from laughing out loud all over again. First Will was just a gorgeous guy in class. Then he was an intensely passionate, amazing kisser. And now she had discovered a comic streak . . . and some kind of melancholy side he wasn't fully able to suppress. Hadn't laughed in a while? What was that all about?

There was something more to Will Simmons than met the eye. And Jessica was looking forward to finding out what it was.

# Lila Fowler

The landscape of Sweet Valley High is changing fast. Anyone with a brain can see that. My friend Jessica Wakefield, however, seems to have put her brain on ice.

Ken Matthews is no longer our school's social leader, and if he doesn't get his butt in gear, his spot on the football team is history. Since Olivia, he's a haunted loner, skulking the halls without making eye contact with anybody, and word is El Carro's QB is primed to take over. Honors classes and school societies are filling up fast with El Carro people. Even in the first week of school the El Carro elite is throwing raging parties and inviting only a select one or two Sweet Valley people. I've heard Sweet Valley wanna-bes whispering about it in the halls.

And then there's Melissa Fox. She is one to watch. And don't be fooled by her passive blue eyes and her fragile look. She's so sharp, it's almost scary.

This is where I get to the part about Jessica. I see her walking into some serious trouble. She's so self-involved, she doesn't see that this guy she's gaga over, Will Simmons, has a girlfriend, and if she knew, she wouldn't see Melissa as a major threat. But I've witnessed too many years of country-club butt kissing not to recognize who's got power and who doesn't.

I'm not going to give Jessica away to Melissa, but I'm not so sure I'm going to warn Jessica either. That may sound mean to you, but you don't know Jessica the way I do. She hasn't stolen your boyfriends, borrowed, lost, or ruined half of your clothes, or charmed your parents so completely that they say things like, "That Jessica certainly works hard at her job—reminds me of myself in high school," in my father's case, or, "Please ask Jessica to come shopping with us today; she has such an eye," in my mother's. It's pretty nauseating.

Jessica and I have an understanding: Only the fit survive. She doesn't need my help, and I never expect hers. Jessica is a survivor; she'll find her way out of this mess.

In fact, knowing Jess, she'll find some way to turn it into a triumph.

Pretty nauseating.

# CHAPTER 6

# Reasons to Worry

"So I told Cherie I had no idea whether Lila Fowler has a sister and to please, for her own good, attempt to buy, borrow, or steal a life as soon as possible." Tia giggled.

"Conner? Conner? *Conner!*"

Conner felt the french fry actually thunk against his forehead before he turned to look at his friend. "What?"

"I hate when you do this." Tia's eyebrows formed a straight line over her eyes.

"Do what?"

"Completely ignore perfectly good gossip. Fail to laugh at any of my jokes."

He smiled. "Sorry, Tee. Could you just hold up your hand or something at the parts where I'm supposed to laugh?"

She gave him the look. The Conner, you-are-a-hateful-miscreant-and-I-don't-know-why-I-stay-friends-with-you look. She started to gather her books from the crumb-strewn cafeteria table. "Does the word *misanthrope* mean anything to you?"

He laughed for real. "Come on, I was kidding. Don't go. I haven't finished my sandwich yet."

She sat down again, but he could tell he was on probation. "Who's that blond girl in the white T-shirt?" she asked.

"How should I know?" Conner answered warily.

"Because you keep staring at her."

Conner tried not to grimace outwardly. Another peril of Tia, besides her tyrannical insistence on having her jokes laughed at, was the fact that she hardly missed anything and *never* missed the things he really, really wanted her to miss.

"I wasn't staring at her. She's in my writing class," Conner stated flatly.

"You were. There's a girl at the cheerleading practices who looks exactly like her, only with shorter skirts and more makeup."

"They're the twins I told you about a few days ago," he said unenthusiastically. Some part of Conner wanted to riff on the absurdity of the Barbie twins and the evil they and their kind represented to high schools all over the country. He could go off. He could use the Tweedledumber line. Tia would appreciate that.

But he just didn't have it in him.

Barbie Two was proving surprisingly hard to mock and ridicule. He hated when people did that. He'd counted on her being stupid and dull-witted. He'd wanted her to say "like" every third word. He'd wanted her to write her essay about her first pet, a poodle named Fluffy. He'd wanted her to shrivel and writhe under his condescending gaze.

Perhaps most of all, he'd wanted her to continue to wear cloying outfits like that awful yellow dress she'd worn the first day and not sensible things like well-fitting jeans and V-necked T-shirts so he wouldn't have to consider the fact that she was actually very pretty.

Over all, Elizabeth Wakefield was turning out to be a huge disappointment.

*I couldn't tell her.*

*I couldn't tell Jessica about Melissa. I was going to. I was going to just tell her when we went out last night. That I had a girlfriend, that I was sorry, and that I wasn't going to break up with Melissa.*

*But when I was sitting there across from her at that restaurant . . . her laugh was so . . .*

*I just couldn't do it. And not
because I didn't want her to get mad
at me, even though I don't. And not
because I didn't want to hurt her,
even though I don't.*

*It was because—and this is the
worst part—it was because I didn't
want to let her go. I want to see her
again. God, I even told her I
wanted to see her again.*

*I guess it doesn't get more selfish
than that, does it?*

Jessica had been dying to talk to Will all day.

Last night at Michael's they'd talked about how the student body would react to the fact that Will had replaced Ken on the team. Obviously the El Carro kids would be psyched, but Will was worried that having a new quarterback would cause a rift. That the school wouldn't be able to get behind him.

Jessica had told him that might be the case if Will had stolen the position from Ken, but that wasn't the way things had worked out. Ken had quit. The SVH students would realize that they were lucky to have a talented quarterback like Will to take his place. But Will hadn't been so sure. He had looked so vulnerable, sitting there in the moonlight.

And now, as of that morning, the word was out. One of the football players had suffered a tongue slip, and now everyone knew that Will had suited up as starting quarterback at yesterday's practice. SVH students weren't reacting quite as Jessica had hoped. There were rumors that Ken had been pressured to quit—that he was still mourning Olivia and hadn't been given a fair shot.

Jessica wanted to find Will and assure him that it would blow over quickly, that she'd cheer for him, that she couldn't care less that he'd replaced a Sweet Valley starter. She wanted to shock her friends by holding his hand as they walked down the hall—she, who almost never deigned to show affection on school grounds for a regular old high-school guy.

She *had* seen him. He was in her history class, after all. The hour she'd lavished on her outfit that morning (white sundress with sweetly romantic eyelet bodice) hadn't gone totally to waste. But he'd arrived at class late and looked at her only briefly before being called away early by a note from the office. Of course he was busy. Obviously he was preoccupied with football at the moment.

Maybe he'd drop a note in her locker before the end of the day.

Suddenly Jessica saw him through the crowd. Will was standing in a doorway at the end of the corridor, and he seemed to be talking to someone in one of the classrooms. Perfect. Will could walk her to her next class.

"Will!" she called, picking up her pace. He didn't turn. "Will!" she called again.

Okay, yelling a guy's name in a crowded hallway was in direct opposition to

Lesson #14: *Never greet a man first.*

But she and Will were beyond rules.

Still, Jessica slowed her steps. Maybe she would just stand here and pretend to tie her nonexistent shoelace or something. Will was in the middle of talking to somebody, and he probably wanted a little privacy when they saw each other. Things between them had gotten pretty intimate pretty fast, and he was obviously uncomfortable showing his heart in public.

Jessica wove through the packed hall, set down her backpack by the wall about five feet from Will, and leaned over. Yep. Her clogs were exactly as she had remembered. Soft, unscuffed, and slightly too small. *One, one thousand, two, two thousand.* The floor was filthy. Gum. Tiny scraps of paper. Unidentifiable bits of . . . something. A guy came flying around the corner and slammed into her side, then mumbled an apology and took off. Jessica barely felt it. At least thirty seconds had passed. The blood was rushing to her head. Will still hadn't noticed her.

*Just talk to him.* She stood and looked up. Will was gone. The corridor was almost empty. Deep sigh. She had blown her chance. Next time Jessica was going to forget the stupid rules of dating.

Besides, hanging back like a wallflower was not in accordance with Jessica Wakefield's most important code:

*Personal Rule #1: Go for it.*

Melissa was scared, but she wasn't ready to show it. She'd show her feelings once she had control of them. That was the way they worked best.

"You got your wish," she said to Will as he stood across from her in the empty, unfamiliar classroom. She wanted to sound genuinely supportive instead of the way she felt, which was nagging and insecure.

He wouldn't meet her eyes exactly. He wasn't moving any closer, though she made sure her body language invited it. He was keeping a secret from her.

She twisted a strand of smooth, dark hair. "I only wish you'd told me sooner so I didn't have to get the word through the gossip network." There was sharpness in her words. It couldn't be avoided.

"I wasn't allowed to tell anyone." His eyes were pointed at her and yet unreachable. She noted the subtle difference between *wasn't allowed to* and *didn't*. Will didn't lie. That made it all the more critical to examine each of his words with care.

For all appearances they were talking about football, but the real issue seemed to scream out for attention. *Who is she? What does she mean to you? Why did you keep her number?*

But Melissa was quiet, and she kept her face composed. The more hysterical she felt, the more important it was to maintain control. She'd learned that lesson the hard way.

She took three steps forward, closing the gap between them. She put her hands around Will's waist, slowly, keeping her eyes locked on his. "I'm happy for you. I really, really am."

He relaxed slightly, but he didn't hold her. "Thanks, Liss," he said. "I really wanted you to be the first to know. I swear." Suddenly his eyes darted left. He seemed startled, and he glanced at the open door. "I have to go. Can we talk about this later?"

Before she could react, he was out of her grasp and nearly to the hallway.

"Will—I . . ." It didn't matter what she said. He was gone. The blood rushed to her face, and she felt her shoulders heave slightly. Will never did that. He never shrugged off her affection. Ever.

There was a girl. Melissa knew it now. Not just some dim-witted admirer. There was a girl who had somehow gotten herself between them, and that girl was going to pay.

"Tia Ramirez seems cool," Enid said to Elizabeth and Maria Slater as they stood by Elizabeth's locker before the sixth-period bell. "Have you met her yet?"

Elizabeth shook her head absently. "Not yet."

"What about Gina Cho?" Maria asked. "She hangs out with that girl Melissa Fox. She's in my sociology class."

"Melissa Fox is the pretty one, right?" Enid asked. "Thin, with dark brown hair? Her locker is near mine."

Maria nodded. "I want you guys to meet Eve Parsky. She's my physics partner. I think she's got a crush on that gorgeous guy, what's his name? Conner?"

Suddenly Elizabeth snapped to attention. "Conner McDermott? You think he's gorgeous?" She didn't mean to sound quite so aggressive.

Maria's eyes widened. "Sorry to offend. But yeah, I think he's amazing looking. So do at least half the girls in my physics class. The guy doesn't exactly bend over backward to be friendly, though, does he?"

Elizabeth tried to seem more casual. "No, he doesn't. He's in our writing class. He and I did not hit it off."

Enid nodded sympathetically. "He's really full of himself. But I have to side with Maria on the looks issue."

Elizabeth shook her head. "I don't see it at all. Maybe if he'd shave, or comb his hair, or wear a decent shirt once in a while . . ."

Maria balanced her books on one hip. "Listen, I've got to go. But Liz, have you decided on the whole fashion-editor business yet? People keep asking me about it, and we need final assignments by Monday."

Elizabeth groaned. "I know, I know."

Ever since Lila had brought up the idea of a fashion column in the *Oracle,* nobody would leave it alone. All the staffers thought it was a great idea. Even their new adviser, Mrs. Halsey, kept bugging Elizabeth about it. "It's just the kind of fun counterpoint we need to all the earthquake coverage," she'd said. Elizabeth couldn't totally disagree. The stories for the first issue were pretty heavy. But she couldn't let Lila onto the *Oracle* either. It would mean giving up her sanity, and was that really worth a few crummy paragraphs on what Jessica wore to the dance?

"So?" Maria prodded.

"I've decided about five times, only nobody will take no for an answer," Elizabeth said unhappily. "I won't put Lila on the staff. I'm sorry if that's unprofessional."

Maria leaned back against a locker. She had a slightly mischievous smile on her face. "Can I propose a solution?"

"Please," Elizabeth said.

"What if you had a fashion editor who wasn't Lila?"

"How could I?"

"Make Lila try out for the position along with anybody else who's interested. It will look just as good on other people's college applications." Maria dropped her voice. "Just make sure the person who gets it isn't her."

"Do you really think I could get away with that?" Elizabeth was starting to feel hopeful.

"It sounds good to me," Enid said.

"I think it's the only fair thing to do," Maria added.

Elizabeth nodded, genuine relief soothing the bunched muscles of her back and shoulders. "Maybe you're right. Lila probably won't even stay in the running. She'll drop out as soon as there's work to do." Elizabeth smiled. "Maria, you're brilliant. You really are."

"Thanks, Liz. Anytime." Maria tried to look modest.

The bell rang loudly.

"Check you guys later," Maria said, hustling off.

"Later," Enid said.

As Elizabeth walked down the hall toward her AP English class, she had to laugh at her own hyperactive conscience. As usual, she'd totally overthought the problem. Lila had probably long forgotten about the whole thing. There was no reason to worry.

Thursday afternoon Jessica scanned the faces of her friends in drama class to make sure they were paying attention. If she couldn't talk *to* Will, at least she could talk about him. She had to do something to make last night's date feel real. She was beginning to worry she'd imagined it.

Amy kept yawning and glancing at her watch, but Annie Whitman and that girl from cheerleading, Tia Ramirez, looked genuinely interested.

"So then Will ordered us a bottle of sparkling cider and we decided to share a dessert . . . ," Jessica continued.

She was sitting on the edge of the stage in Sweet Valley High's high-tech auditorium, getting in as many words as possible before Ms. Delaney showed.

"And then he just leaned over the table and he—"

"Uh, Jessica?" Tia interrupted.

"Yeah?" She really hated to break off when she was just getting to the good part.

"I was wondering . . . are you talking about Will *Simmons?*" Tia asked.

Jessica grinned. "Tall, knee-weakening looks, new quarterback of the Sweet Valley High football team, Will Simmons."

"Oh." Tia had a strange expression on her face.

"Off the stage, Jessica," Ms. Delaney called from the back of the auditorium. "Gossip time is over."

Jessica jumped from her perch and slid into one of the seats in the front row of the auditorium. Drama was one of the few classes that actually held her interest—and Ms. Delaney was tough. If Jessica wanted a decent part in the school play this semester, she was going to have to play by the rules during class.

"Today we're going to talk about soliloquies," Ms. Delaney said. "Who can tell me what one is, for starters?"

Easy one. Strictly middle-school drama class. Jessica felt a sharp elbow in her back as she was about to raise her hand. "Jess, for you." Amy thrust a folded piece of notebook paper onto her lap.

Jessica unfolded the note as she half listened to Maria give the definition of a soliloquy.

JESSICA,
I DON'T KNOW YOU THAT WELL, BUT YOU SEEM LIKE A NICE PERSON. BEWARE: WILL SIMMONS HAS A SERIOUS GIRLFRIEND. SHE HAD MAJOR POWER AT EL CARRO, AND I'M SURE SHE WILL HERE TOO. STAY AWAY FROM WILL. TRUST ME ON THIS.

TIA

Jessica read the note twice before the words actually entered her brain. Then she stuffed the note in her bag and swallowed back the sick feeling that was rising in her throat.

It couldn't be. Will didn't look at her like a guy who had a girlfriend. God knows he didn't kiss her like one.

Tia had to be mistaken. Confused. Or maybe she was jealous.

Jessica shook her head to clear it. Realistically,

Tia didn't seem jealous. She didn't seem confused either.

*What if it's true?* Of course it could be true. Plenty of guys cheated on their girlfriends—it happened every day of the week. And she had known, deep down inside, that there was something weird about the way Will seemed so guarded, so strangely tentative one second and passionate the next.

*It can't be true,* a voice in her head cried out. *What happened between us felt so real.*

She suddenly felt like she was going to throw up. Her hand was raised before she realized it.

"Jessica?" Ms. Delaney asked.

"May I be excused to the bathroom?" she choked out.

Ms. Delaney looked concerned. "Yes, of course."

Jessica clutched her stomach as she hurried out the door and down the hall. She barely made it into a stall before she threw up. She staggered to the sink and turned on the cold-water faucet full blast. She splashed her face again and again. When she looked up at her reflection, it was red and splotchy.

She wasn't going to cry. She'd avoided crying for a long time now, and it would be dangerous to start. She knew from experience that the best way to stop the hurt was to get mad, and she had good reason to be mad. Will had misled her. He had told her he wanted to see her again. He had kissed her with an intensity that held the promise of something real. And she'd believed he was a guy who kept his promises.

She was wrong. He was a liar and a user and a jerk. He was just a hell of a lot better than most guys at making her believe he was something more.

She cringed at the memory of the things she'd said about their future together. She must have seemed so desperate to him, so pathetic. The worst part was he'd tricked her into letting down her guard, into really *hoping,* and hope was a nasty habit she'd thought she'd kicked.

The tears were getting close now. She had to focus on her anger before they came and drowned her.

She remembered another rule. One she hadn't needed to use before.

Lesson #99: When a guy blows you off, blow him off worse.

She needed to take action. That would help. Revenge was action.

# Ken Matthews
# on Football

Sometime between Olivia's death and now, male-bonding rituals started to turn my stomach.

It's not like my teammates haven't tried to be supportive. Everybody, including Coach Riley, has said at least once, "I want you to know how sorry I am, Ken. . . ." But seriously, do they even care? Do they know that Olivia was a brilliantly talented artist? Do they care that she happened to be one of the nicest people ever to grace this planet? Do they care that Olivia's eyes got darker as the day turned into night?

Of course not. They care about football. They care about saying the things that will make me quit acting like some kind of ghost and get with the program.

Coach Riley actually said to me, his hand on my shoulder, his gaze steady and serious, "I know it's been hard, Ken, but you've still got your place on this team as starting quarterback." I am not joking. That was the most profound comfort he could think to offer.

So does he <u>really</u> think that playing quarterback on a high-school football team is going to make me feel better? Does he actually believe I'm going to sleep easy tonight knowing that sure, my girlfriend is dead—but gee, I still have my place on the team?

The answer? Yes. He really does. That's what it means to be a football player.

That's why Coach Riley has dedicated his life to the sport and why I quit the team.

# Get Angry

**7**

Layout. Check. Circulation. Check. Ad sales. Check. Personal Profiles columnist. Check. Sports editor. Check. The list went on and on. *Check. Check. Check.* Elizabeth couldn't believe that the *Oracle* staff was really coming together. After only four full days of school, she was beginning to believe they might actually put out the first issue of the school newspaper on schedule. Amazing, considering her nerves were fried.

She'd spent almost the whole of last night listening to a blaring state-of-the-art stereo. Lila liked to listen to a top-forty station when she got in bed and often fell asleep without turning it off. When Elizabeth had finally fallen into restless sleep around four in the morning, her dreams intermingled with stupid song lyrics. *Next time I'm just walking into her room and smashing the thing,* Elizabeth decided.

Today was the day to resolve that final piece of the puzzle. Elizabeth pushed her chair away from her official editor-in-chief desk and stood up.

"Can I have everyone's attention, please?" she called.

About a dozen people had been hanging out in small groups, discussing article ideas. Immediately they all turned around and looked at her expectantly. *I sort of like that,* Elizabeth admitted to herself. She suddenly imagined Conner McDermott sitting in the meeting. *Would he think of me as more than a vapid blond who wears colorful clothing that was recently washed and doesn't have holes?*

"Yeah, Liz?" Maria prompted. "Do you have an announcement?"

Elizabeth crashed back to earth. "Yes." She couldn't help glancing toward the door. Her spies had told her that Lila was at the cheerleading meeting with Jessica, but leave it to the world's soundest sleeper to burst in at the worst possible moment.

"We have a new position on the *Oracle*," Elizabeth announced. "Fashion editor." She noticed several kids glance at one another. "As you probably remember, it was Lila Fowler's suggestion," Elizabeth continued. "But I think the most logical way to assign the position is to give anyone who's interested the opportunity to write a sample column. Please help spread the word, and I'll tell Lila myself when I get home. Ask all interested parties to have their samples in my box by two tomorrow. I know it sounds like a tight deadline, but meeting tight deadlines is what being an editor is all about. I'll post the winner tomorrow afternoon."

"Cool!" Jen Graft, an enthusiastic (if somewhat annoyingly perky) sophomore exclaimed.

Elizabeth paused. "That's it—we'll make it a short meeting today. Thanks, everybody, for such a productive first week."

Elizabeth plopped back into her chair and rubbed her eyes. The dark circles had been so bad this morning, she'd seriously considered borrowing Jessica's concealer. But even the most expensive brand wouldn't conceal the fact that her face looked drawn and her cheekbones a little too sharp and prominent. She wished she didn't feel responsible for joining her parents at the Fowlers' dinner table so many nights a week. She wished she could be more like Jessica and blow it off.

Maybe tonight she would eat at Maria's house and get some rest. Maybe Lila and Jessica would want to get their beauty sleep for a long week of pretryout practices. Yeah, right. They would probably play hip-hop tunes into the wee hours to practice their dance moves.

"Elizabeth?" Megan Sandborn had appeared next to Elizabeth's desk.

"Hi, Megan." She smiled. "What can I do for you?"

Megan smiled back shyly. "I—I wanted to know if I could help you with proofreading next week. I was a proofreader on the El Carro paper last year. You look like you could maybe use a little extra help."

Elizabeth laughed. "I look that bad, do I?"

Megan's eyebrows shot up, and blood rushed to her cheeks. "No, no, not at all! That's not what I meant. You look great. I only meant . . ."

Elizabeth held up her hands. "Don't worry, I know you didn't mean that. Really." She smiled at Megan reassuringly. "It's just that you're right. I haven't been getting a lot of sleep lately."

Megan nodded. "I'm sure being editor in chief is pretty nerve-racking."

"Yeah, that and other stuff . . ." Elizabeth's voice trailed off.

She certainly hadn't planned to burden Megan with her domestic situation, but the girl continued to stand there with a look of empathetic encouragement that Elizabeth knew too well. Only she wasn't usually on the receiving end of it.

"It's nothing, really," Elizabeth explained. "Just that my family was invited to move in with the Fowlers until our house was fixed, and I guess . . . well . . . they have a different lifestyle than I'm used to and Lila is . . . well, anyway. I have no reason to complain."

"Could you live somewhere else?" Megan

106

asked, clearly sensing all the things Elizabeth wasn't saying.

Elizabeth thought for a moment. "Oh, I've thought about it. Believe me. But my friend Enid lives in a small apartment with just her mom, and most of my other friends' families have given their extra rooms to other displaced people. Besides, in the first few weeks after the earthquake I think it was really important to my parents that we all stay together."

Megan nodded thoughtfully. "Can I make a suggestion that might sound totally crazy?"

Elizabeth shrugged. "Sure."

"Well, I'd need to talk with my mom and everything ... but ..."

Elizabeth was starting to suspect where Megan was going with this. She knew she should turn her down right away, but the girl looked so genuine and eager that Elizabeth didn't want to hurt her feelings.

"We have a nice, big guest room that no one's using," Megan went on in a rush. "It gets a lot of sun, and it's really quiet. My grandmother used to live there," she explained. "We had a couple staying there right after the earthquake, but they moved back into their own place about a month ago. My mom was just saying the other day that it's a waste with no one using it...."

Elizabeth jumped in before Megan could go

on. "Listen, it is really, really nice of you to offer, but—"

"Just think about it, okay?" Megan asked. "Will you at least think about it?"

"I don't know. . . . I—"

"Because you would actually be doing *us* the favor," Megan added quickly. "My brother drives me to school most days, but I hate always depending on him for everything and . . ."

Megan looked so hopeful, Elizabeth knew this was no meaningless invitation. She could see in Megan's eyes that the girl really *wanted* Elizabeth to stay in her home. Maybe she was lonely.

In spite of herself Elizabeth was starting to fantasize. Peace. Quiet. Independence. "What about your brother?" she asked. "He probably wants his privacy."

Megan shrugged. "Trust me, when he wants his privacy, he knows how to get it," she said with a laugh. "You wouldn't be in the way."

Hmmm . . . this was getting tempting. But her parents would be disappointed. How could she leave them alone at that cold mansion? And what would the Fowlers say?

"I promise I'll think about it," Elizabeth said. "And no matter what, I really do appreciate the offer."

She gathered her things, feeling better than she had in days. Maybe she would bring it up with her parents just to feel them out. Maybe they'd understand how much it would mean to her. And if not? Well, it was nice just thinking about it.

Jessica was pacing outside the locker rooms before cheerleading practice. Up past the water fountain and back down to the bulletin board. Up and back. Up and back. She had to deal with this now. She couldn't carry the rage back home with her.

After drama class she'd strengthened her stomach for a little information gathering, and all the news was bad news. Tia had not been confused. Far from it.

Yes, many people were aware that Will had a girlfriend. Her name was Melissa Something-or-other. And yes, he had been dating said girlfriend since the beginning of time. And no, there were no rumors that the couple's relationship was on the rocks or that Will had cheated on her before.

Jessica's breath quickened as she heard the door to the boys' locker room ease open. It was him. Her first bit of luck all day.

"Will." She said his name before she lost her nerve.

He saw her, and he couldn't pretend he hadn't.

"Jessica, hi." He had that wary look. He ought to.

"I need to talk to you," she said coldly.

"I have practice. This isn't a good time." He was firm, but not nervous.

"I don't care," she said, trying hard not to let her voice rise toward the hysteria clawing her throat.

"Jessica, let's talk later," he said evenly.

"You have a girlfriend," she stated before he could walk away.

Will nodded. At least he wasn't a coward.

"You have a serious girlfriend, and you have no plans to break up with her." It was testament to her pitiful state that Jessica actually hoped he would deny this statement.

Will nodded again.

She was starting to lose it a little. Her throat was closing around her voice. "Why did you do it? Why did you lead me on? You told me you wanted to see me again. Did you think you could have us both?" Her words were choked and openly emotional. She hated the sound of them. *Not pain. Not hurt,* she ordered herself savagely. *Anger. Get angry.*

He was starting to move away. He didn't want a scene. Other guys were spilling out of the locker room and obviously noticing the tension in the air.

"You are such a liar, Will," she hissed. She didn't care that anyone heard. Why should she protect him? "You are a cheating, using liar."

Several guys were listening. Will's jaw was clenched so tight, it looked like his molars would crumble.

110

"Go back to your girlfriend," Jessica nearly shouted. "If she'll put up with you cheating on her, she must need a boyfriend in the worst way."

Practically the entire football team was assembled now. No one was moving.

She needed the last word. Her dignity depended on it. She turned on her heel. "I'd rather kiss the toilet bowl in the locker room than kiss you ever again," she raged over her shoulder.

She was gratified by the few snickers she heard behind her as she strode off. They were just enough to keep the tears from spilling over.

## TIA ON CHEERLEADING AS A FEMINIST PURSUIT

WHY IS IT THAT PEOPLE THINK IN ORDER TO BE A FEMINIST, YOU HAVE TO BE INTO GUY THINGS? YOU HAVE TO BE A JOCK. YOU HAVE TO BE A CAREER WOMAN. YOU HAVE TO "WEAR THE PANTS." STAYING HOME TO RAISE THE KIDS IS OUT. WEARING PINK IS TOTALLY OUT. AND BEING A

CHEERLEADER, WELL, DON'T EVEN
GO THERE.

I CONSIDER MYSELF A
FEMINIST. I AM ALSO A MINISKIRT-
WEARIN', POM-POM WAVIN',
CARTWHEEL TURNIN', VARSITY
CHEERLEADER. AND I'M DAMN
PROUD OF IT.

I'M SICK OF ALL OF THESE SO-
CALLED GIRL-POWER PEOPLE
TELLING ME THAT THERE'S
SOMETHING DEMEANING ABOUT
CHEERLEADING. THEY SAY
CHEERLEADERS PROJECT A
NEGATIVE IMAGE OF WOMEN
BECAUSE WE STAND ON THE
SIDELINES AND CHEER FOR THE
BOYS' TEAMS. APPARENTLY
UNLESS A GIRL IS OUT THERE
PLAYING BASKETBALL OR SOCCER
OR TENNIS, SHE ISN'T A REAL
ATHLETE. I INVITE ALL SKEPTICS TO
JOIN IN ON ONE FOUR-HOUR-LONG

STUNTING PRACTICE. THEN COME TO
ME WITH YOUR RIPPED-UP
KNUCKLES, BRUISED SHOULDERS,
PULLED HAMSTRINGS, AND
TWISTED NECK MUSCLES AND TELL
ME I'M NOT AN ATHLETE.

AND BY THE WAY,
CHEERLEADERS SERVE A
HIGHER CAUSE. IT'S CALLED
SCHOOL SPIRIT. THOSE GUYS
OUT ON THE FIELD ARE OUR
FRIENDS (MOST OF THEM
ANYWAY), AND WE LIKE GIVING
THEM SUPPORT.

I BELIEVE THAT BEING A
FEMINIST MEANS PURSUING YOUR
GOALS, WHATEVER THEY MAY BE,
AND NOT LETTING ANYONE—MALE
OR FEMALE—STAND IN YOUR WAY.
WHETHER THAT MEANS PULLING
ON A PAIR OF OVERALLS AND
GOING TO WORK ON A BUSTED
CARBURETOR OR STRAPPING ON A

TUTU AND DANCING WITH
BARYSHNIKOV. AS LONG AS
YOU'RE ACHIEVING AND STRIVING
TO IMPROVE, YOU'RE ONE
SUCCESSFUL WOMAN.

MY NAME'S TIA RAMIREZ AND
I'M A FEMINIST. I'M ALSO A
PROUD WEARER OF MINISKIRTS.
SO SUE ME.

"Elizabeth, honey, is that you?"

Elizabeth heard her mother's voice only moments after she'd plodded up the stairs, following an exhausting shift at House of Java. Funny how she used to love the smell of roasted coffee beans. Now it clung to her like her bad humor, stronger and more acrid the wearier she felt.

The coffeehouse was one of the few hangouts that hadn't been turned to rubble by the earthquake, so it was always packed. Today she'd been jumpy through her whole shift, hallucinating that Conner McDermott was sitting at practically every table or about to appear behind every customer in the long line.

"Yeah, hi, Mom." She detoured into the room where her mom and dad slept. It seemed like her mom spent more and more time in there.

Probably the only place in the house where her mom felt any sense of privacy or control.

"I just got the strangest phone call," her mom explained, looking up from the many design magazines, books, and sketch pads piled around her on the floor. Elizabeth almost wanted to laugh. As huge as the house was, her parents used this relatively small space as bedroom, living room, den, study, and occasional dining room.

"Yeah?" Elizabeth asked, sinking down on the bed. Her mom's face showed even more tension than usual.

"It was a woman named Eleanore Sandborn. Apparently you know her daughter?"

"Megan," Elizabeth said. She knew where this was headed, but she didn't say anything.

"She told me how much Megan admires you, which I thought was very nice of her," Mrs. Wakefield continued. "But I thought it was an odd reason for calling a person out of the blue."

"Mom, I . . ." Elizabeth's voice trailed off.

Her mom took a breath and plunged onward. "But then she told me that she was calling to invite you to live at their house for the next few months. She said you and Megan had already talked about it. Is that true?"

Elizabeth could see the look of hurt that had worked its way over her mother's features, and it made her feel awful. "No, I mean, well, yes. Megan did mention it to me. But I didn't tell her I would or anything. I told her I'd think about it. I didn't want to hurt her feelings."

"Did you tell Megan you weren't happy here?"

Ugh, more guilt. Elizabeth couldn't find it in her heart to say that she *had* indicated she wasn't happy. That in fact she had totally underplayed it because she was more than unhappy, she was miserable. But she couldn't tell her mother how horrible she'd been feeling. The last thing her parents needed was more stress. "No, Mom. I just . . . I just think Megan could really use the company."

Her mother seemed to consider this for a few moments.

"I know this isn't easy on any of us, Elizabeth. But we are very, very fortunate the Fowlers have been generous enough to house all of us together. They feed us and take care of us and won't take anything in return. So many families are . . ."

Elizabeth tuned it out. She'd heard the speech before. She'd *given* the speech before.

So much for her parents' understanding. She was stuck here until the far-distant future when the Wakefields' house was finally reconstructed. She had to deal with it. She had to stop being such a baby. Because if she looked on the bright side, life at the Fowlers' probably wouldn't get any worse.

# Lila's Fall Fashion Advice: Sample Fashion Editorial

Fashion is important. People judge you on what you're wearing. So listen up, guys and girls. I've got a few things to say.

First of all, boots and skirts don't belong in the same outfit. And don't wear white after Labor Day. I don't care how hot it is outside. Just don't do it! Also, don't believe the hype about knockoffs. If you can't afford the real thing, forget it.

For the huge number of you who think that seventies fashion is cool, I have some news. It's not. I don't want to see any bell-bottoms. Put away those pathetic double-knit shirts—in fact, throw them away; they won't be coming back into style. Here's a phrase that's easy to remember: Polyester is never okay.

A special word to you girls who hang out on Upper Field during lunch: The Gap is not the only store in the world. I know it sounds scary, but there are alternatives out there. Try another store. I know you can do it.

And I'm afraid there's only one thing to say to you guys in the <u>Star Trek</u> shirts who sit in the right-front corner of the cafeteria: Seek help now.

Shopping is a full-time job. If you're going to be hip, you've got to commit yourself. Go to the mall every day and look for sales (if you need to buy stuff on sale, that is). Read fashion magazines. Or at least look at the pictures. Real style takes work.

I like to pick out what I'm going

to wear to school the night before. That way I don't have to rush around in the morning. You all might want to follow my lead in that department. I've seen a lot of people at SVH who look like they just put on the first thing their hand hit in the closet in the morning. Believe me, it shows.

I guess that's all for now. You can thank me later—after the halls of Sweet Valley High are no longer such a fashion nightmare.

The End

# CHAPTER
## A Pile of Lies
8

Jessica was talking too much. Words, thousands and millions of them, sprang from her mouth. She released them into the air without thinking. That's how she got sometimes when she was feeling overwrought.

She was sitting amid a cluster of cheerleading hopefuls in the courtyard during lunch period. She hadn't touched the basil, tomato, and fresh mozzarella sandwich provided by the Fowlers' kitchen staff. She hadn't taken a sip of her diet Coke. That would require shutting up for several seconds in a row.

". . . So I told him off in front of the whole football team . . . ," she babbled. "I hadn't meant to. We were alone at first, and then they all came pouring out of the locker room. So what could I do? He was hating every minute of it. You really should have seen his face. . . ."

She was talking so obsessively, she hadn't even realized that a couple of other girls had ambled over and joined her group. El Carro girls, the one with the blue eyes and the red-haired one.

"I told him I'd rather kiss a toilet bowl than kiss him again," she continued, barely pausing for breath. "It was pretty harsh, but I'm telling you, the guy deserved it. He's a liar, and I feel sorry for the poor pathetic girlfriend who probably follows him around like a little sheep. Think about it. What kind of head case would stay with a guy who abused her that way?"

None of the girls seemed ready to supply an answer, so Jessica went right on. "I mean, he's good-looking, sure, but nothing so special." That was a lie. She thought he was one of the most swoon-worthy guys she'd ever laid eyes on, but truth wasn't the point right now.

Jessica looked up. Lila was shooting her death looks. Oh, so what? She'd spent so many hours listening to Lila moan about guys, she was sure she'd built up some credit in that account.

"And the guy can't kiss worth a damn," she went on. That too was a lie. His kisses affected her in ways she'd never imagined possible.

"I'm over it, and I'm glad to be done with him," she said, tossing a third lie on the pile. "The last thing I need is a lying, cheating loser, and that's what Will Simmons is. He and his loser girlfriend belong together. I hope they live pathetically ever after."

She heard a muttered word and then the crinkling

121

of papers. She looked up to see the ice-eyed girl jump to her feet. The girl looked ill. She walked away quickly, followed by the redhead.

Jessica shrugged. "I guess that girl has a weak stomach for gossip."

Lila let out a long, impatient breath. "Jessica, why don't you shut up for a minute or two? I think you've done enough talking."

Elizabeth stuck her fork into the piece of veal on her plate. How could she make it look like she was eating this poor baby cow without actually ingesting any?

"I had a meeting with my new client today, Mrs. Cortez," her mother was saying. The soup bowls had been cleared away just minutes before, and already her mom was filling the silence with boring shoptalk. "I showed her my initial sketches for the living room, and she seemed very pleased. She's such a nice woman and so easy to work with. . . ."

*Conner McDermott would probably think that picking out wallpaper and fabric swatches for a living was beyond meaningless,* Elizabeth found herself thinking, and then instantly hated herself for it.

"I know Lucille Cortez," Mrs. Fowler said. "Is she redecorating the whole house or just the one room?"

"We've only talked about the living room so far. . . ."

Lila yawned hugely without bothering to hide it behind a hand. *You are an awful person,* Elizabeth thought sharply, hoping her mother hadn't noticed. Lila was just plain rude, and the fact that Elizabeth was having traitorous thoughts of her own only made it harder to take.

No doubt Lila returned the sentiment. When Lila wasn't being bratty to Mrs. Wakefield, she was casting evil looks at Elizabeth across the table, and Elizabeth had a pretty strong suspicion as to why.

Elizabeth had chosen a fashion editor, and it wasn't Lila. She'd actually laughed out loud when she'd read Lila's submission, but not because she thought it was good. It was so singularly snotty and mean-spirited, Elizabeth knew she wouldn't run into resistance from anybody when she rejected it. Well, not from anybody whose opinion she respected.

Besides, Jen Graft had turned in an intelligent, *purposely* funny, worthwhile editorial. Elizabeth had read every single submission and kept coming back to Jen's. Hiding behind that ingratiating demeanor was one witty writer. This afternoon Elizabeth had posted a notice that Jen had won the position, even though she knew it would throw Lila into dull tantrum mode. From Lila's behavior this evening, it was obvious she'd seen the announcement.

Elizabeth's mother and Mrs. Fowler must have said absolutely everything they could have about Mrs. Cortez's living room, because she realized everyone was completely silent. Awkward, awkward, awkward. Elizabeth pulled her eyes away from Lila's accusatory stare and studied her sister, who'd picked tonight to make one of her rare dinner appearances. Jessica was tearing apart a piece of French bread as if she were murdering it.

Jeez. Somebody had to say something. Anything.

"So how are things at the *Oracle*, sweetie?" she heard her father ask. "Is the staff coming together the way you had hoped?"

Elizabeth's stomach tied itself in a triple bowline. Anything but that.

"It's, uh, going okay. Everything seems fine." Her voice was squeaky and weird. She was desperately hoping the conversation would end there.

Lila held up her fork as though she were going to stab Elizabeth with it. "It's all fine and great except that Elizabeth stole my idea," Lila spat.

No one seemed to want to follow up, so Lila plunged ahead. "I came up with the idea of fashion editor for the paper. Of course Princess Elizabeth said *nooo*, the newspaper didn't need a silly fashion editor. She'd rather get a B on a math test than let stupid Lila Fowler anywhere near her precious *Oracle*. But the rest of the staff and the faculty adviser loved the idea. So what does Elizabeth do? She steals my idea and appoints somebody else!"

Forget about awkward. This was so far beyond awkward that even the oblivious George Fowler looked sick to his stomach.

"Lila, I—," Elizabeth began.

"She appointed a *sophomore*," Lila interrupted. "There aren't any other sophomore editors, are there, Liz? You chose her just to rub my face in it, didn't you? Be honest for once."

Elizabeth felt her shoulders tighten, her stomach roll. "I chose her because she handed in the best sample article."

"Yeah, right!" Lila screeched. "That dweeb?"

"Lila, please," Mrs. Fowler said. She looked even more horrified than the three other parents.

Jessica was smashing each and every one of her peas with the blunt end of her butter knife.

"Elizabeth, maybe you should rethink your decision," her mother said calmly. Great. Her own mother wasn't even supporting her.

Elizabeth opened her mouth and closed it again.

"Why aren't you saying anything, Liz?" Lila barked. "Are you too ashamed of *stealing* my idea to even try to defend yourself?"

Elizabeth inhaled, exhaled. *I can't do this,*

she realized. *I just cannot do it.* She stood up from the table. "Mr. and Mrs. Fowler, thank you very much for dinner. I hope you won't mind if I excuse myself."

Grace Fowler shook her head. She was too stunned to blanket the awful moment with social pleasantries. "Of course not," she said.

Elizabeth left the room with as much composure as she could muster. She marched up the stairs and down the long hallway to her room.

Then she threw herself facedown on the scratchy chintz bedspread and cried.

## Sample fashion editorial
## by Jen Graft
## Ignored by the Back-to-School
## Fashion Industry: The California
## Story

It's September. A time for changing leaves and chilly breezes. A time for pleated wool skirts and cardigan sweaters. A time to bring those thick cords and turtlenecks out of storage.

If you live in New Hampshire.

Why is it that those of us who hit the books in the State of Perpetual Summer are completely ignored by every reputable fashion magazine? Is it because they're all produced in New York City, where the sun is a thing to be feared, loathed, and blocked at all costs? Or do high-fashion editors actually think that we're all such slaves to trends, we'll wear those thick ribbed stockings till our thighs sweat off?

What we really need is a California-based fashion magazine that caters to the fashion-minded, yet naturally tan teen. But until the day that Condé Nast launches <u>Beach</u> <u>Teen</u> magazine (and if they call it that, none of us will buy it), we're going to have to take care of ourselves—show the world that we shoreside Californians have our own back-to-school style.

So forgo forest green, navy blue, and burgundy. Break out the cargo shorts, miniskirts, and Birkenstock sandals. Turn those cords into cutoffs, always, <u>always</u> wear a bathing suit under your school gear, and keep the board in the back of the car. After all, the guy or girl with true California style is always ready for anything—especially the karmic call of the perfect wave.

Except . . . ahem . . . if that wave calls during school hours, because then, of course, you will have to wait until classes are out for the day.

Well, kids, I'm outta here. Until next week, happy shopping!

Melissa tapped on the sliding-glass door that opened into Will's room. She needed to talk to him in private, and she wasn't going to hazard a meeting with his mom at this hour.

He appeared at the door a few seconds later. He was shirtless, wearing sweatpants tied loosely at the waist. He didn't look surprised to see her. "Liss," he said.

She walked past him into the room. The lamp above his desk was on, but otherwise the room was dim. She didn't want to sit on the bed. That signaled intimacy. She sat stiffly in his desk chair.

She kept her eyes down. He was trying to read her face, and she didn't feel like letting him yet. "I know about Jessica," she said. She wrapped her arms around herself. She was shaking.

Will nodded as he sat on the bed across from her. "I figured that was what this was about. What did you hear?"

"Does it matter? Why don't you just tell me?" She lifted her eyes now. Let him see how puffy and bloodshot they were. Let him see what he had done.

Will kicked at the floor. He changed his position on the bed. "Jessica came on to me. That's the truth."

Tears were slipping down Melissa's cheeks. Little shudders skated along her spine.

Will looked pained. Worried. Good, let him worry. He tried to lean close and put his hand on her cheek, but she slapped it away.

"Did you kiss her?" she choked out.

Will threw his hands in the air. "The girl's a troublemaker, Liss. Can't you see that? She's been out with practically every guy on the football team. They all had stories to tell about her. She targeted me as her next conquest, and she got pissed when she found out I had a girlfriend." It wasn't an answer.

"But did you kiss her?" Melissa was really crying now. Heaving, sobbing. Will looked scared. The muscles in his face and neck were so tight, they ticked.

He leaned on one hand. He leaned on the other. He sat up rigidly straight. He dropped his eyes. "No."

Melissa allowed herself a steady breath. She wiped a hand across each eye. He'd never lied to her before. She knew that. But then, she'd never had to confront him about a girl before. Would he lie to her to avoid a fight? Did she really believe him? Or did she just want to believe him?

He got up from the bed and retrieved some toilet paper from the bathroom. He handed it to her, and she blew her nose. He knelt before her, circled her waist with his arms, and rested his head on her lap.

Whether or not Will was lying, Melissa decided to let it go. One thing was certain, Melissa wasn't about to let a girl—any girl—come between her and Will. Maybe he had been tempted, but he was human. She knew he loved only her, and she wasn't going to lose him now.

Melissa ran a hand gently through his hair, but she wasn't thinking of its softness or shine. She was thinking of Jessica Wakefield and how deeply she hated her.

Elizabeth had finished with her tears and was laying facedown on her bed when she heard the knock on the door half an hour later.

"Uh-huh?" she said into her blanket.

"Elizabeth, may I come in?"

"Sure, Mom," she said, her words muffled by the bedspread.

"Elizabeth?" Her mom opened the door slowly and peered in. She came quietly over to the bed and sat down.

Elizabeth rolled over. Her mother placed her hand on Elizabeth's forehead and smoothed back her hair.

"Are you okay?"

"Yeah. I'll be fine." She knew her mom needed her to say that, so she did without thinking.

"Elizabeth, honey, your father and I had a little talk, and we agreed that if you'd really like to move in with Megan Sandborn—even just for a week or two—we'll accept it. It's obvious you aren't happy here. And if you and Lila aren't getting along, there's no reason to force you both to live together."

Elizabeth felt her spirits begin to scrape themselves from the soles of her feet. "Really?"

"It's not what we'd hoped for, but . . . well, nothing about this earthquake is what anyone hoped for. . . ." Her mom's face was lined with sadness, and her eyes looked dull and distant.

Elizabeth was quiet. Her mom stood up and started to straighten the pillows on Elizabeth's bed.

"Why don't we visit the Sandborns tomorrow?" her mother suggested cheerily. "If you like the feel of it, we'll go ahead and make arrangements. How about that?"

Elizabeth gave her mom a wobbly smile. "That would be great."

She wished her mother would open up enough to confide in her about how hard the last three months had been. Elizabeth would love to bond over shared stories of the crushing Fowler household and the things they missed about home. It would have been such a relief to get to say all those things out loud and to know her mother was feeling the same way.

But that just wasn't her mom's style. And Elizabeth was going to have to live with that.

# Megan Sandborn Finally Gets a Sister
## (Well, Sort Of)

Elizabeth Wakefield is coming to live with me.

Elizabeth Wakefield.

Could my life get any better? I've always wanted a sister. When I was little, I used to wish for one all the time, but then my parents split up and it was pretty obvious <u>that</u> wasn't happening. But now Elizabeth is moving in, and she's, like, a dream sister. She's a great writer and she's so, I don't know, put together. She's one of the coolest seniors at school. And she's so easy to talk to. I mean, there's stuff that a person wants to talk about that . . . well . . . let's just say having a big brother isn't always sufficient.

Like the first time I had to go buy . . .

um . . . feminine products and my mom was dead asleep on the couch. I ended up sitting in the bathroom for about three hours until one of Mac's girlfriends found me and loaned me something. Then, of course, she told him all about it, and Mac felt the need to "have the talk." I think it was the most humiliating moment of both our lives.

Mac is just such a guy. He's totally cool, of course. The best. And I know he and Elizabeth are going to love each other. Well, not love, love . . . But then again . . .

# CHAPTER

# Backstabbing 101

"There they are," Melissa murmured to Gina and Cherie, steering them through the skylighted corridor of the mall. It was one of the few places in the valley that had been left largely untouched by the earthquake.

It was one o'clock on Saturday afternoon, and Lila Fowler and Amy Sutton were standing in front of the window of Bebe's, studying a pair of leather pants. Melissa was relieved it had taken such a short time to find them.

"Lila, Amy, hi!" Melissa said brightly. Gina and Cherie were right behind her.

The two girls turned around. Lila looked a little surprised at Melissa's upbeat friendliness. She could tell Lila was scanning her face for signs of fallout from yesterday's drama. She wouldn't find it.

"So are you guys getting ready for the big night?" Melissa asked easily. "The leather pants are very cool, by the way."

"That's what I think," Amy said, giving Lila a satisfied look. "We were just arguing over them."

"I say go for it," Gina suggested.

"Listen, we're heading over to Melrose day spa for manicures and pedicures," Melissa explained, "but I'm actually really glad we ran into you. A bunch of us are getting together for a predance thing on the beach over by Mariner's Point. It's kind of an El Carro tradition."

"Matt Wells and Josh Radinsky made a point of asking me whether you two were going to be there," Cherie added, naming two of Will's best friends, both extremely desirable.

Amy's face glowed. Melissa knew she was a simple target. A few well-placed words would make a personal slave out of Amy Sutton. It was Lila's face she studied carefully. Lila would suspect the ramifications here.

"Sounds like fun," Amy chirped. "What time?"

"Seven, seven-thirty?" Melissa suggested.

Lila was still quiet, thinking.

"What about you, Lila?" Cherie asked.

Lila slung her sleek square bag over her shoulder. "Am I right in assuming that Jessica Wakefield is not invited?"

*Good for you*, Melissa thought. *I'm impressed.* Melissa had been keeping her expression impassive, but maybe she'd allow a tiny smile. It was a moment for confidence. "I'm sure you can understand why Jessica would not be my favorite person right now," Melissa said evenly. "So, no. I'm not going out of my way to invite her." This bit of diplomacy was more for Amy's benefit, a little balm for the girl's conscience should it ever appear.

Lila remained silent. She was holding out. That was fine.

"We've really gotta go," Melissa said, no sign of care in her face or voice. "We'll be at Melrose if you feel like stopping by."

"So we'll see you at the beach?" Cherie asked.

Melissa sent a telepathic thank-you to her friend. She was glad it was Cherie who asked the question.

Lila thought for another moment. She obviously saw exactly what the answer to this simple question would mean. Melissa could see the two sides playing themselves out in Lila's mind. Stand by her best friend, make an enemy of Melissa, and destroy her future social status? Or betray her friend, win Melissa's loyalty, and gain instant acceptance into the El Carro crowd?

*Which will it be?* Melissa asked silently. *Choose your fate wisely, Lila.* Melissa glanced at her watch. Her face gave nothing away.

Lila tapped the toe of her glossy leather boot on the ground. She switched her bag to the other shoulder. "I'll see you there," she said.

Melissa rewarded Lila with a genuine smile before she turned to go. *Good answer.*

\* \* \*

Four boxes. After seventeen years on this planet all of Elizabeth's worldly possessions fit into four large cardboard boxes. *At least that makes it easy for me to move,* she reasoned.

Just an hour before, she and her mom had returned from a very successful visit at the Sandborns'. Megan was incredibly sweet and welcoming. Mrs. Sandborn seemed as if she'd just stepped out of the latest issue of *Good Housekeeping,* almost too good to be true. She was attractive and charming and said all the right mother-to-mother things. It turned out she and Mrs. Wakefield even knew each other vaguely from some garden committee or other. Mrs. Wakefield was delighted that the house was just over the hill from the Fowlers', not even a ten-minute drive. The place was big and sunny and tastefully decorated with a lot of overstuffed and slipcovered things. Nice, but not too nice. Big, but not too big. No servants, thank God.

Elizabeth wasn't totally sure about the status of Mr. Sandborn. She got the impression they were divorced and that he lived in another city. But his absence didn't appear to bother Mrs. Wakefield.

Although the brother wasn't there, Elizabeth felt confident he would be as nice as Megan and her mom. She racked her brain for a guy named Sandborn in any of her classes. He was probably shy like Megan. She pictured light hair and an open face. He was a senior too, Megan had said.

Elizabeth felt her tensions easing and her excitement growing. She would sleep. She would eat. She would do her own laundry. She would walk the halls without fear of evil mutterings from Lila. No one would make her drink Perrier.

Suddenly the world seemed like a much lighter, happier place. She would finish packing this afternoon and drop most of her stuff off at Megan's, come back here to get dressed for the dance tonight—maybe even get to spend a little time with her impossible-to-find sister if she was lucky—and then move into Megan's house tomorrow morning. Simple.

"But first, there's the question of what to wear to the dance," Elizabeth said aloud. She walked to the closet, where several of her dresses were still hanging. She needed to leave out her clothes for tonight and something to change into tomorrow.

There was the short, pale yellow dress with the spaghetti straps. The long, navy linen skirt and matching tank top. A black miniskirt. A long-sleeved, silk, flowered blouse. She was leaning toward the miniskirt. The yellow minidress was definitely out. Conner McDermott would think she was a dork.

Wait a minute—Conner's opinion of her should not factor into her wardrobe decisions. Since when did Elizabeth let a guy affect her image? She pulled the dress over her head and went over to study her appearance in the mirror.

Truth was, she did look dorky. The dress was too conservative, even with the short length. And taking her hair into account, there was just too much yellow. She pulled it off and left it in a little heap on the floor.

Elizabeth reached for the black miniskirt and pulled it up over her hips, then stepped back and admired the cut. Conner probably wouldn't even be there. But what if he was? It wouldn't hurt anyone if she looked drop-dead gorgeous, right?

Suddenly Elizabeth had an idea. She searched through her boxes for a black silk camisole. Jessica had given it to her as a present last Christmas and then borrowed it several times, but Elizabeth had never worn it. She slipped the weightless fabric over her head and then turned back to her closet. She found a sheer, slightly shimmery, wine-colored blouse. At the time she hadn't known what possessed Jessica to buy it, but in Elizabeth's current mood it felt perfect. Sophisticated and sexy. With a pair of open-toed black sandals and a little burgundy lip gloss, she'd be set.

*If Conner McDermott happens to like this outfit, then that's not my fault, is it?*

"You look beautiful, Jess," Elizabeth said as they pulled the Jeep into a parking spot in front of the Sweet Valley High gymnasium Saturday night.

"*You* look incredible, Liz. Seriously. Tonight I'm not at all sorry to know I look exactly like you," Jessica replied.

Elizabeth switched off the ignition. "Thanks. The feeling's mutual."

Jessica sighed before opening the door. She did feel sexy tonight. She'd helped herself to Lila's closet, choosing a short red dress with a zipper that went almost from the top to the bottom. It was the least Lila could do after having stood her up without a word tonight. They had made specific plans to give each other facials and drive to the dance together. Where was Lila anyway?

Jessica felt a little black cloud gathering over her mood, and she pushed it away. This was a night for feeling good. She'd dance with a whole bunch of different guys—all and any who asked. Dancing always made her feel better. She'd show Will and his mouse of a girlfriend, Melissa, whoever she was, that she had come through the whole disaster unscathed. The way she looked in this dress, she hoped Will would take a good, long eyeful and deeply regret what he was missing.

"You ready?" Elizabeth asked.

Jessica could tell by Elizabeth's concerned look that her sister knew something was up. But she could also tell Elizabeth wasn't going to make her talk about it until she was ready. That was one of the many reasons Jessica loved her sister. She couldn't blind Elizabeth with a lot of self-hyping bravado the way she could other people. Elizabeth would see the hurt almost immediately, and Jessica didn't want to talk about that.

"Yeah," Jessica said.

Elizabeth still didn't open the door. "By the way, thanks for letting me take the Jeep this week."

Jessica smiled and shrugged. "No biggie. I'm sure Mom's idea of switching off every other week will work. And if not, I'll just make Dad buy me a new car."

Elizabeth laughed. "Right. I have a feeling you're going to have plenty of reasons you absolutely *have* to have the car when it's my week to drive it."

"Come on, Liz. I'm not *always* a self-obsessed jerk," Jessica said.

"I do not—," Elizabeth started to protest.

"I know! I know!" Jessica said. "I was just kidding, Liz. You're one of very few people who focus on my positive points, and I really appreciate it." She felt her eyes filling, so she cracked open the door before Elizabeth could respond. "Let's do it."

They set out across the parking lot. The far horizon still glowed with the last fading ribbons of sunset.

"I'm going to miss you when you move."

"Jess, you're *never* home," Elizabeth protested. "This way I'm going to make you have lunch or coffee or dinner with me a couple of times a week. I'll see you more than I did before."

Elizabeth looped her arm around Jessica's waist. Jessica did the same. They hadn't walked like this in months, and it made Jessica smile.

"We are going to *dominate* this year," Seth Hiller said as he crushed a tin can between his palms.

"We will now that we've got Simmons at QB the way it should be," Matt Wells added.

"El Carro!" Will cheered.

Melissa laughed as Will knocked fists with each of his friends. "The way it should be," she repeated as he came up behind her and wrapped his arms around her waist, pulling her into the midst of his little crowd.

Melissa smiled contentedly and leaned back against Will's chest. The warmth of the bonfire felt familiar and comforting, but not nearly as comforting as the warmth of Will's body pressed against hers. Melissa looked around at her other friends, some huddled in couples and others participating in little gossip circles. She took a deep breath of the smoky air and let it out slowly. This was the way it should be. The regular El Carro faces had come together at Mariner's Point just as they always had. Standing here, cuddled up with Will, listening to him talk football with his offensive line, Melissa could almost convince herself that SVH didn't exist.

"Melissa, thank you so much for inviting us." Amy Sutton appeared at her side along with Gina and Cherie. Amy grabbed her wrist in that slightly annoying, feel-like-I've-known-you-forever way. "Lila and I had the best time."

"I'm glad," Melissa said sincerely.

"This girl has a wicked sense of humor," Cherie told Melissa. "Amy, someday you have to tell her that story about the blackout in the locker room." Cherie held her stomach as she laughed.

"Oh, totally," Amy said. "You guys should come over one day this week after practice. I'll get my dad to make his monster brownies and I'll dish you all the Sweet Valley dirt worth dishing."

"I'm there," Gina said.

"Sounds good to me," Melissa agreed.

"Hey, Liss." Will planted a kiss on top of her head. "We should really get going to the dance."

Melissa glanced around and saw a bunch of kids making their way up the beach toward the parking lot. Matt and Marcus Seiler were starting to douse the fire. Melissa felt a momentary twinge of regret, as if she were waking up from a good dream.

"Where's Lila?" Melissa asked.

"Making up for a summer of celibacy," Amy said with a sly grin. She gestured over her shoulder, and Melissa looked past her into the shadows. Lila was in a good old-fashioned lip lock with Josh Radinsky. Ah, Josh. Melissa knew he'd pick Lila out of the crowd. She was exactly his type. Beautiful, aloof, and wearing an outfit that probably cost more than Will's car.

"Maybe we shouldn't interrupt them." Melissa smirked.

"I'll take care of it," Will said. "Hey, Rad!" he called at the top of his lungs. "Break it up!"

Melissa and the rest of her friends laughed as Josh tumbled off the piece of driftwood he and Lila were seated on.

Lila stood up and offered Josh her hand. "Need some help?" she asked, causing another round of laughter. Melissa liked this girl. She liked Amy. And they both seemed to be finding their niche within the El Carro crowd. This evening was going perfectly.

And it was only going to get better. Because in less than an hour, Jessica Wakefield would know exactly who Will Simmons belonged to.

Melissa squeezed Will's hand as he navigated their way across the darkened beach. She smiled as he squeezed back, imagining Jessica's expression when she and Will walked into the gymnasium together. Suddenly Melissa was very much looking forward to this dance.

# Dance Chairperson
## Maria Slater's
### "Welcome Back" Speech

All right, everyone, I'll keep it short and sweet. This dance is an old Sweet Valley High tradition. It's meant to bring everyone back into the school spirit after a long summer of lazing around, defining tan lines, watching soaps, and working brain-numbing jobs at the Quik Chek. But this year the Welcome Back dance has taken on new meaning. This is our chance to come together as a school—for El Carro guys to dance with SVH girls and vice versa. For all of us to ease the tension that we all know has been brewing. Remember, people, we are going to have to live with each other for at least a year.

So let's all take a cue from that group of guys in the back who have been partaking in a communal helium suck fest since the night began. I want to see some serious mingling. Hey! I've even given you your opening line. "Who's that annoying girl up there on the stage who won't shut up?" (Pause for possible laughter.)

So greet your neighbor, have a good time, and thank you for your undivided nonattention. (_Note_ _to_ _self:_ Leave stage before it sinks in that everyone _was_ actually ignoring you.)

# CHAPTER 10
## Carefully Chosen Clothes

Jessica glided through the open door of the gym and paused. Elizabeth had stopped outside to chat with some friends, leaving Jessica to make her entrance alone, which was fine by her. She tugged on the bottom of her extremely short dress (which, incidentally, still had its tags when she'd pulled it from Lila's closet). The place was packed. And it was dark. *So much for my grand entrance.* She would go to plan B. *Hit the girls' rest room, accept admiring compliments from whoever happened to be there, and head out to the dance floor armed with the evening's gossip.*

Jessica walked to the bathroom, gently swinging her hips and humming along to a slow song. A few days ago she'd imagined herself dancing cheek to cheek with Will Simmons to a ballad like this. *By the end of the night I'll have danced with five guys even cuter than Will,* Jessica promised herself.

The girls' room was crowded, as Jessica had expected. There was something about school dances that caused all the girls to gravitate toward harsh,

147

unflattering fluorescent lights and wall-to-wall mirrors.

"Hey, everyone!" Jessica called, announcing her arrival to the general female populace. She wanted to make sure everyone got a good view of her (or rather, Lila's) killer dress.

The chatter stopped. Eight girls turned and looked at her. Six of them turned away—almost in unison. There was one quiet hello from a Sweet Valley girl she barely knew. No you-look-awesomes. Even Sophi Maillard, whom Jessica had talked to during the first cheerleading meeting, didn't bother to call out a greeting. Weird. Jessica glanced down at herself. Had she accidentally left her dress unzipped? Had her skin turned purple somewhere between Lila's and here? Had she sprouted a zit? What?

She glanced in the mirror. Everything on her person was as it should be. *"Hello!"* Jessica repeated.

Sophi turned away from the mirror. "Uh, hi, Jessica." Her voice was low, almost a whisper.

"Ooookay," Jessica muttered, backing out of the rest room. There was a very strange vibe in that place. A vibe that was in no way enhancing her party mood. It was probably because there were so many El Carro girls hanging around. They were intimidated by her or something. They were uncomfortable with the new surroundings.

148

She would have to tell Lila about this. Then they could stand in the corner and make fun of the El Carro girls (when they weren't busy dancing). Jessica ambled across the gym, heading in the general direction of a group of girls she recognized from drama class.

"Jessica Wakefield! Nice zipper!" The remark had come from a guy Jessica had never seen before.

"Easy access!" another guy said snidely. She recognized that one. He was on the football team. She remembered him from the hallway outside the locker room. What a jerk! Who did he think he was talking to? Was she supposed to be drawn to him by that sleazy comment?

Jessica kept walking. She wasn't even going to deign to respond to those guys. She passed a tall brunet—cute, but not so cute that he'd have an attitude. She slowed down to give him a chance to ask her to dance. But all the guy did was jab his friend in the ribs and whisper something. She heard them both laugh as she passed.

There was definitely something bizarre in the air tonight. Jessica was getting attention, all right. But not the kind of attention she wanted—or was accustomed to. She needed to find Lila immediately . . . and find out what the hell was going on.

*Why am I nervous?* Elizabeth asked herself as she walked toward the gym at a pace so slow that she was almost motionless. *I'll go into the dance, hang out with my friends, talk to a few El Carro people, maybe dance if anyone asks.*

Was she worried about seeing Todd under these circumstances? *No,* she answered herself, and she knew it was honest.

But there was a guy she kept imagining seeing everywhere. *Are you worried about seeing Conner McDermott?* she asked herself. *No,* she answered even faster, but this time it didn't feel so honest.

So she was nervous about seeing him. It wasn't all that strange. They'd had two extremely unpleasant encounters and one . . . well, she wasn't sure how to sum up the encounter in class when they'd read each other's essays out loud. It was natural for her to be nervous about walking into another round of insults.

He probably wasn't here anyway. He wasn't the type to show up for a school dance. He was home, writing political manifestos for some weirdo web page. Maybe he was drinking black coffee at a diner and saying mean things to unassuming girls with lipstick and carefully chosen clothes. He definitely wasn't here.

And if he was, she'd just pretend she didn't see him. No problem.

Well, she'd arrived at the door to the gym. Miniskirt falling a little low on her hips. The buttons of her blouse fastened. Yep. Right shoe on right foot, left shoe on left. Yep. So it was time to go inside.

Elizabeth stepped through the door. It took only seconds for her to locate a group of her friends: Maria, Enid, Brooke Dennis, Todd, Aaron Dallas. They were standing near the punch bowl. *I'll just take a quick look around before I join them,* Elizabeth reasoned. She wasn't nervous about Todd, but at the same time there was no point in exchanging awkward dialogue with him when she didn't have to.

Elizabeth circled the gym, sticking close to the wall, where she had the best view of the crowd. There was Jake Collins and Max Waters. She saw Lionel Jenkins and Annie Whitman.

A tall, dark-haired guy was walking toward her. Her heart thudded. Nope. Not Conner. *Admit it, Wakefield. You're looking for Conner.* But only so she could be sure to avoid him, she comforted herself.

Elizabeth had made a full circle. No Conner. *Maybe he's in the bathroom. Or hanging out in some dark corner.*

She waved to various people she knew. She walked toward the punch bowl. Todd was already dancing with some El Carro girl. Maria was waving her over. She smiled brightly.

"Hey, you look gorgeous!" Maria said.

"Thanks, so do you," Elizabeth said, suddenly

feeling that it didn't matter very much whether she looked gorgeous or not.

As she greeted her friends and listened to them chat over the loud music, reality settled over her. Two realities, actually. First was that Conner McDermott really hadn't come to this dance. Second was that Elizabeth was disappointed.

It was strange, sick, and inexplicable, but true. She wanted to see Conner. She wanted Conner to see her. She wanted to trade insults with him if they couldn't think of anything else to talk about.

She closed her eyes, and when she opened them, the room seemed to rock and sway. Why was she wanting him like this? She hated him. He hated her. She didn't even think he was that cute.

Okay, he was that cute. When being honest, might as well be honest.

But he thought *she* was laughable looking. He'd expressed that in a lot of different ways. He would never like her. Ever.

When had her brain completely lost control of this situation? She thought back. It happened when he'd read her essay. When she read his. When he smiled at her. He might style himself after Sid Vicious most of the time, but when he smiled that day, he looked like . . . God, she didn't even know what he looked like.

Crazy as it was, for the first time in her life she had a crush. She, Elizabeth Wakefield, a girl so levelheaded even *teachers* came to her for advice, had a crush. She knew about them, of course. Her friends had them all the time. But in truth, she hadn't really understood the concept of a crush until tonight.

And it didn't feel good. It felt like a stomach flu mixed with PMS mixed with too much caffeine. It felt like her heart and her mind weren't even on speaking terms anymore. Worst of all, she had a sinking premonition that nothing short of a heart transplant was going to get him out of her system.

No, she couldn't accept that. She'd fight it, and she knew how. She might have lost her mind, but she still had her self-discipline. She'd avoid him. She'd stay as far from Conner McDermott as possible until this awful malady passed.

# Melissa Fox on Surviving the Pitfalls of Childhood

Cherie Reese has been my best friend since the second grade, except for our one minor breakup in fifth grade. I used to go to her house every single day after school because that was when my sister was too cool to hang out with me and was busy making my life hell. (Hiding my Barbie dolls, locking up her makeup, convincing my brother it would be way fun to pop out on me in the dark whenever possible.) But at the Reeses' we always had peanut-butter-and-jelly sandwiches cut into triangles and we'd sit in the basement in old beanbag chairs and pretend we were princesses in thrones. We'd even make her little sister bring us goblets of milk. There we were in charge, and Cherie and I were inseparable.

In October my fifth-grade class went on a field trip to the zoo, and on that same day I got chicken pox. I missed the trip, and then I missed another week of school. When I came back, everyone had made a zoo animal for this big collage on the back wall. Cherie and a bunch of other girls in my class were gathered back there, whispering about something, and I went over to join them. That was when Renee Talbot called me "scab face" and everyone laughed. Everyone, including Cherie. Then Renee pulled Cherie over to her table, and I had to sit with the boys.

The estrangement lasted for about a week. Then I started talking about my birthday party and how fantastic and fun it was going to be and how my mom and sister were going to give everyone makeovers. All the girls, including Cherie and Renee, started playing with me at recess, picking me first for kick ball, and sitting at my table during art. On the day I brought my invitations to school, Cherie helped me hand them out. Everyone but Renee got one. She was pretty crushed.

But what could I do? My

mom told me I could only have
fifteen girls, so I had to choose
carefully. Some things just can't
be helped.

# CHAPTER
## Sharing a Bathroom

This was stupid. There was no reason why Jessica should feel self-conscious about the fact that she happened to be standing all alone. She was Jessica Wakefield. She could stand by herself anytime she felt like it. Still . . . where was everybody? Where was Lila? Where was Amy? Why wasn't she collecting her usual crowd of friends and admirers?

*Everyone is here . . . somewhere.* Jessica stood uneasily at the edge of the gymnasium's large, makeshift dance floor, scanning the crowd. This was getting ridiculous. Jessica was willing to forgive Lila for blowing her off earlier—sometimes her best friend had an overwhelming need for a manicure or a massage that couldn't be put off. But Lila didn't even seem to be here. If the girl was lying bloody in some ditch, having flipped her Porsche, Jessica was going to kill her. Lila *never* wore her seat belt. Never.

*Lila is not in a ditch,* Jessica told herself. Maybe she had gotten a really awful haircut, and she was at this very moment shopping at an all-night wig store. And she had probably recruited Amy to go along for moral support. Yeah. It had to be something like that . . . which still left Jessica standing by herself.

Okay, she was getting desperate. Everyone had those moments . . . it was nothing to be ashamed of. Jessica would do what she always did when she didn't know what else to do. She would go talk to Elizabeth and her less than scintillating friends. They were standing near the punch bowl, chatting earnestly, although she noticed Elizabeth was staring off into space, looking mildly nauseated. Even Elizabeth probably had her limits for long discussions of whether a 93 percent on a test was really an A or an A minus.

She started to walk toward her sister, then paused. A slow, romantic song started. Jessica looked up, hoping to spot a friend on the periphery of the slowly moving couples. It was always easier to find people when the whole crowd wasn't gyrating and jumping around.

She couldn't quite process what she saw. She suddenly felt strangely out of time and place. Most of her senses felt deadened. The sounds of the dance had resolved themselves into a low buzz in her ears. But her eyes were perfectly sharp. She saw Will Simmons with his arms wrapped snugly and protectively around a slender, graceful-looking girl. Jessica should have turned away for her own good, but she didn't. She watched the couple sway rhythmically to the music, rotating slowly until Jessica's eyes locked on the eyes of the girl. The Girlfriend. Big, light blue, ice eyes. She was the girl from cheerleading. The girl who'd listened to her bash Will in the courtyard and left in a hurry. Jessica saw a lot in those eyes. She didn't see a sheep or a loser or a desperate wimp. She saw pure, intense hatred, and it was focused on Jessica.

*She had major power at El Carro, and I'm sure she will here too. Stay away from Will.* Jessica had to hold her breath to keep herself from letting her intense dread show through on her face as she remembered Tia's note.

*Get out of here!* Jessica screamed at herself. She needed a few minutes alone to think about what this meant, to regroup, to figure out how to deal. Instead she stood frozen, pinned by the haunting eyes of her enemy.

Melissa smiled and tilted her head back so she could look up at Will. He automatically looked down at her and kissed the tip of her nose. She almost felt bad for Jessica, standing there in that tasteless red dress at the edge of the circle.

*She'd have to be blind not to see how much Will loves me,* Melissa thought. Jessica was trying not to look affected and failing miserably.

But at this moment Melissa couldn't feel bad.

Not when she and Will were moving together so perfectly as they had so many times before. Not when he had that look in his eyes. That look that told her he knew her, knew her inside and out and loved every last not-quite-perfect inch. That look that told her he'd always be here, watching, protecting.

Melissa cast one last look in Jessica's direction, but the girl had disappeared. All the better. Let her go off and lick her wounds. Melissa was satisfied that her message had gotten across. Now she wanted to be alone with Will. And that was hard to do with thwarted boyfriend poachers gaping at her from the sidelines.

Elizabeth stood in a shaft of morning sunlight on Sunday in the middle of her new bedroom, absorbing every detail of her surroundings. She couldn't have imagined a more perfect place to spend the first semester of her senior year in high school. The floors were polished hardwood, the walls painted a pale aqua. In the corner of the room—next to a picture-perfect bay window— was an unadorned pine desk.

Things felt so different in this room, in this light. It felt like a place to collect herself and regain her sanity. It was a room that didn't invite obsessive thoughts about boys who didn't like her.

"Do you like the room, Elizabeth?" Megan's

voice broke into Elizabeth's thoughts. "Is it okay? I hope you won't mind sharing a bathroom. My brother's room connects on the other side."

Elizabeth smiled at her new friend. "I *love* it. It's perfect. And trust me, I'm used to sharing a bathroom. Are you sure your brother won't mind sharing with *me*? I mean, I'll try to keep all my girlie stuff out of his way."

"Don't worry about it." Megan grinned. "He's not going to have to cart me around everywhere I want to go. He'll be so grateful for that, he'll never notice a few more bottles around the sink."

"A symbiotic relationship," Elizabeth commented. "The best kind."

"I'll go get us something to drink," Megan offered. "Go ahead and make yourself comfortable."

Elizabeth nodded as Megan darted from the room. She was mesmerized by the floor-to-ceiling white linen curtains that hung from the room's three large windows. Even now, in the morning sunlight, the curtains were billowing in the breeze. She couldn't wait to personalize the room with her books and clothes and pictures. As she peeled the tape off a cardboard box labeled Bath and Shower, Elizabeth felt the stress of the last couple of weeks melting away. She would unpack her toiletries, then take a long, hot shower. Megan had placed fluffy white towels on the huge four-poster bed in the middle of the room.

Then maybe Elizabeth would take a nap. The bed looked so inviting, and she didn't have to work until four o'clock this afternoon.

Elizabeth pulled shampoo, conditioner, soap, and a kiwi facial scrub from the box. *Or maybe Megan and I can do a spa day,* she thought as she headed toward the door that connected her room to the bathroom. Elizabeth really could use some pampering and relaxation, and Megan would probably like it. Sort of a big-sister, little-sister activity . . .

Elizabeth nudged the bathroom door open with her foot and walked in.

"Hey—" It was a male voice. An angry one.

Elizabeth sucked in her breath. She tried to back out of the small room, but the door had closed behind her and her arms were full.

Time stopped. The shower curtain was thrown open. Elizabeth dropped every one of the things she was holding.

He was wet from the shower and wearing only a towel around his waist. She was hyperventilating.

Conner McDermott glared at her in angry astonishment before he stole the words right from her lips. "What *the hell* are you doing here?"

Do you want to know why I didn't go to the dance last night? (Aside from the fact that I hate school dances and never go to them?) I didn't go because I <u>wanted</u> to go. Sound strange to you? Welcome to my world.

I wanted to go because I wanted to see Barbie Two. Did I want to see her because I wanted to laugh snidely at her clothes and her friends and the way she danced? I would like very much to believe so, but I am not a liar. I didn't go to the dance because I did not want to want to see her. At all.

So how do you think I felt when I discovered, less than an hour ago, that the earthquake charity case my sister brought home, the stray puppy who will be sharing my life, my home, my mother, my sister, and my <u>bathroom</u>, for God's sake, is none other than Elizabeth Wakefield?

# ELIZABETH WAKEFIELD

## 11:04 A.M.

Could I sleep in the Jeep for the next few months? Could I afford Motel 6? Who do I know with an extra sleeping bag?

# JESSICA WAKEFIELD
## 11:22 A.M.

The red dress is lying on the floor next to my bed, so I guess that means last night actually happened. Before I opened my eyes, I was hoping it was a nightmare. Who am I kidding? It <u>was</u> a nightmare — only it was the waking kind. The kind with consequences.

That girl is evil. I can sense these things.

So why is he in love with her?

Why?

I don't care. I don't.

## 11:30 A.M.

But I still want to know why.

# WILL SIMMONS

## 11:33 A.M.

I'm lying in my bed, thinking about Jessica Wakefield. Not the kind of thoughts you're imagining. Trust me. I'm thinking about the fact that I lied. I'm thinking about the fact that I said some things to the football team that I shouldn't have. I'm thinking about the fact that Melissa is spreading lies and rumors about her and I'm not correcting them. I'm thinking about how dark and rotten my soul feels right now.

I'm thinking about the fact that after all that's happened, I'm still thinking about Jessica Wakefield.

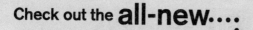

# RULES & REGULATIONS FOR THE MEET

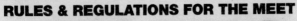

## SWEEPSTAKES

### I. HOW TO ENTER:
NO PURCHASE NECESSARY. Enter by printing your name, address, phone number, and date of birth on a 3" x 5" index card and mail to: *NSYNC* Sweepstakes, BDD BFYR Marketing Department, 1540 Broadway, 20th floor, New York, NY 10036. Entries must be postmarked no later than March 15, 1999. LIMIT ONE ENTRY PER PERSON.

### II. ELIGIBILITY:
Sweepstakes is open to residents of the United States and Canada, excluding the province of Quebec, who are 18 years of age or younger as of March 15, 1999. The winner, if Canadian, will be required to answer correctly a time-limited arithmetic skill question in order to receive the prize. All federal, state, and local regulations apply. Void wherever prohibited or restricted by law. Employees of Random House Inc. and BMG; their parent, subsidiaries, and affiliates; and their immediate families and persons living in their household are not eligible to enter this sweepstakes. Random House is not responsible for lost, stolen, illegible, incomplete, postage-due, or misdirected entries.

### III. PRIZE:
One winner and a friend, accompanied by a parent/legal guardian, will "win a date" with *NSYNC* (date and location to be determined) consisting of a private lunch with the band, a question and answer session, and the opportunity to take photographs (approximate retail value $1,000). Transportation and food provided by BDD BFYR. All other expenses are not included.

### IV. WINNER:
Winner will be chosen in a random drawing on or about March 30, 1999, from all eligible entries received within the entry deadline. Odds of winning depend on the number of eligible entries received. Winner will be notified by mail on or about April 15, 1999. No prize substitutions are allowed. Taxes, if any, are the winner's sole responsibility. BDD BFYR RESERVES THE RIGHT TO SUBSTITUTE PRIZES OF EQUAL VALUE IF PRIZES, AS STATED ABOVE, BECOME UNAVAILABLE. In the event that there are an insufficient number of entries, BDD BFYR reserves the right not to award the prize. Winner's parent/legal guardian will be required to execute and return, within 14 days of notification, affidavits of eligibility and release. A noncompliance within that time period or the return of any notification as undeliverable will result in disqualification and the selection of an alternate winner. In the event of any other non-compliance with rules and conditions, prize may be awarded to an alternate winner.

### V. RESERVATIONS:
Entering the sweepstakes constitutes consent for the use of the winner's name, likeness, and biographical data for publicity and promotional purposes on behalf of BDD BFYR with no additional compensation or further permission (except where prohibited by law). Other entry names will NOT be used for subsequent mail solicitation. For the name of the winner, available after April 15, 1999, please send a stamped, self-addressed envelope to: BDD BFYR, *NSYNC* Sweepstakes Winner, 1540 Broadway, New York, NY 10036.

# Win a Date
## with
# ★NSYNC!®

Kick back with Justin, J.C., Lance, Chris, and Joey!

Here's your chance to hang with mega-hot band ★**NSYNC**, up close and in person! One lucky winner will get the chance to have a very special lunch with the band and conduct their own private interview! See rules for details.

BFYR 203